HELEN OF NOWHERE

Makenna Goodman is the author of two novels, *Helen of Nowhere* and *The Shame*, and has written for international publications including the *New York Review of Books*, the *Los Angeles Review of Books*, *Harvard Review*, *The White Review*, *BOMB*, *The Common*, *ASTRA Magazine* and *Mousse Magazine*. Also an editor, she is based in Vermont.

'Virtuosically written, with an insanity inside its sanity – or the other way around – that seems the proper use to make of reality in this moment.'
— Rachel Cusk, author of *Parade*

'Goodman has wrought an epic in miniature, somehow as appealingly vast as a Greek tragedy or a Platonic dialogue, equal parts philosophy and art that's also delightfully wicked, like something from a fairytale or a fever dream.'
— Sarah Manguso, author of *Liars*

'A furious energy runs through *Helen of Nowhere*, whose every sentence is a joy to read. This is a book about loneliness and bitterness written with a wicked humour, and its moments of grace are as striking as they are enigmatic. A unique and brilliant work.'
— Ayşegül Savaş, author of *The Anthropologists*

'*Helen of Nowhere* is an extraordinary book, gripping, daring, and unusual. With a pacing that completely swept me along, Goodman explores the need to steady oneself by valuing that which is dear, by taking care of the love that needs to be nourished. The trajectory through anger into healing feels like a real journey in time – the dialogue flashing past, written with such speed and brilliance. I wolfed it down.'
— Celia Paul, author of *Letters to Gwen John*

'*Helen of Nowhere* is one of the most surprising novels I've ever read. Goodman has found a unique way of blending political urgency and psychological insight with an almost hallucinatory spiritual dimension.'
— Vincenzo Latronico, author of *Perfection*

'*Helen of Nowhere* expands one's sense of how a novel can be written.'
— Sheila Heti, author of *Alphabetical Diaries*

'Uncanny and brilliant in its voicing of power and control, excellent on what it means to come face to face with one's own hubris, be that literary, philosophical or embodied. An intimate and immersive tour de force by a writer with a fearless style.'
— Preti Taneja, author of *Aftermath*

'Never have I read a book before that seemed to me so much like a dream, both utterly strange and somehow my own. A jolt, a bracing gasp of air, this is a novel for anybody who has had the thought recently that all contemporary fiction is the same.'
— Polly Barton, author of *What Am I, A Deer?*

'Blending biting wit and gorgeous lyrical prose, *Helen of Nowhere* is at once a modern satire summoning Dickens in *A Christmas Carol*, an exploration of the failures of second wave feminism, and a sneaky ode to Woolf and Thoreau. It's hard to pin down what this book is exactly, and whether or not Helen is Jesus, a furniture maker, God, the house, a wife, or time itself. Which is why you must restart it the moment you turn the last haunting page.'
— Alexandra Auder, author of *Don't Call Me Home*

Fitzcarraldo Editions

HELEN OF NOWHERE

MAKENNA GOODMAN

for TMK and JFK

CHARACTERS

MAN, late fifties, wool buttoned vest, arborist-style pants with a worn-in notebook crease in the back pocket, lives in the city.

REALTOR, forties, attractive hippie type, selling a house in the country.

HELEN, seventies, hardscrabble but aging well, owner of the house.

WIFE, forties, in a sunny apartment in the city.

ACTS

1. MAN

2. REALTOR

3. HELEN

4. HELEN AND MAN

5. WIFE

6. MAN AND WIFE

ACT 1

MAN

I think it's okay to tell a woman she's beautiful once a year. Any more than that and her life will be about being beautiful, entirely. Anything less and she'll feel a lack of love and attention. My wife always said I never told her she was beautiful enough. But like I said, I don't think it's good for women.

Someone told me that life is a collection of details you choose to pay attention to. Most of my life has been taken up by my work, but since my work has always been about observing nature, I consider my life's work all about paying attention. This is what I told my students: The world is to be observed, and observing for its own sake is a life worth living.

The house, for example, was warm, despite its being unfurnished, with simple wooden features and beams containing echo strokes of a handheld chisel. There was a built-in couch with a dark blue fabric cushion, its edges sewn by hand, somehow both right-angled and arched in a crescent shape. Beside it, an ornate cast-iron wood stove. The windows were large, single-paned. There was a piece of upright wood in the corner, a gnarled tree or trunk that had been elevated into something sculptural. Besides that, nothing but gleaming, empty space.

I was in the middle of nowhere. I was looking for a simpler life. I had driven all day, alone, to get there.

Everything had become so useless and vast, like acres and acres of lodged wheat.

My life had been lived in tune with one philosophy, which was this: within nature exists the divine. That's all. And because the tools of human construction have warped the meaning of things like songbirds, it is the work of teachers—and people—to remove our constructions, and upon their removal, invoke our innate ability to engage in simply *being*. Nature is the teacher, not I, is what I always told my students.

I built my department from scratch around this beautiful idea. We read and wrote, but the greatest work of all was to remove ourselves from the politics of the city and allow the voice of nature to speak to us, through us. Through the act of such communion, our own true nature might reveal itself. We wrote for ourselves and also as a way to translate nature's teachings for others. It was enough to witness the patterns of plants, the footprints of deer, the movement of grasses in the wind. This witnessing led to the transcendence of the human spirit.

My program was lauded for its experiential approach, and as such, funding was never hard to find. For years we cultivated a transformative practice through a curriculum combining time spent in natural spaces with the study of texts left by humble thinkers who spoke lovingly of the earth and the desires of the heart. I would take students out to wild places around the city, separate them, and alone they would observe, for three full days and two full nights with basic food and rudimentary shelter—no matter the weather or risk—the divine relationships in nature and the thoughts that were born.

Time passed.

And with it came a new generation of teachers.

Women, who were critics, and who encouraged others to be critical too.

Critical of me, among other subjects. Of my work. I don't think I am wrong to say that they took a special pleasure in criticizing my field of interest.

Who is allowed to feel at home in this so-called nature, they asked, and what are the conditions informing the peace provided to those people by the simplicity I espoused? The new generation of teachers said that my approach to teaching was a purity test, the imposition of ritualized discomfort in nature as a means of cultivating virtue.

They questioned my methods.

They rejoiced to find in my hunt for simplicity and silence a complexity of ambition and prejudice.

But in their own hunt for complexity, they were oversimplifying.

I had nothing against women.

In fact, I loved women. I'd worked hard for women my entire life.

It just so *happened* these new teachers were women. I swear it didn't factor at all into my disdain for them. I didn't like to think of myself as a man, even, as I was so much more than just man. But they were times of taxonomy.

One of these women accused me of overidentifying with my work. She was a writer who gave a captivating performance at faculty meetings. I found her prose was good at the sentence level, but her vision was still developing. She pointed out problems with my thinking. She wanted to discuss everything on a structural level. Our colleagues found her funny. She was magnetic, self-absorbed, convincing in her beliefs, arrogant in her delivery, annoying, reductive. She interrupted me, she disliked me.

She was successful, widely praised.

And she was close friends with my wife.

Three years, and I had been drinking.

My wife was, at one time, a very beautiful woman. But over time, her beauty faded, and with it went her desire for me. There were so many years of notoriety that had held us together, my success, her adoration, my appreciation, the agreements we had made.

It likely wasn't fair of me to see her beauty as fading, it would have been fairer to see it as maturing, and yet if I'm being honest it really did look to me as though it were withering not ripening.

At first the changes in my position were devastating, even though they were largely ideological. It wasn't violent, but quiet. My wife and I would weep gently in each other's arms.

And yet with time, the lower I felt, the brighter she became, though to me that brightness felt punishing, like exiting a theater at midday.

I had lost everything. And at the beginning, she felt she had lost everything too. It was a shared loss that at first brought us closer together. There wasn't a way for us to remain viable without my career, we told ourselves. It was what provided us with an excuse to remain in tandem. The university was our container, it was where we had met, it was where we had formed.

But I had died.

That is, I became dead. To the world, and to me.

And yet she was alive, my wife said.

Her dog enjoyed my spot on the bed.

She would caress it while I lay far out, pushed to the edge. Such gazing, such devotion. She would invite it onto the blanket and rub its long, blond ear.

Early in my career I taught a nature-writing class to a small number of students, each of whom was meant to research a plant that interested them.

Every meeting we would discuss a different student's work by performing a collective interrogation, all of us asking one student questions rapidly in succession about their plant and their pasts as a way to access something deeper. The student in question would become flustered and exposed, providing an opening for their subconscious to emerge. These questions and answers, paired with a botanical inquiry into the plant they had chosen, culminated in a lyrical theory of each student's driving inquiry, which was eventually revealed. This aided them in their writing—it gave them a root.

One of my students was beautiful.

Although I didn't look at my students through the lens of desire, it was impossible not to notice her beauty, and I did so objectively.

She chose for her plant, *Gomphrena*, a tender annual with lovely, papery, globelike heads. Called the amaranth of poets, this flower was considered the emblem of immortality, and was said to have been worn by the Thessalians at the funeral of Achilles. If cut before fully ripe, tied in bunches and hung upside down to dry in the airy dark, *Gomphrena* would retain its color for the entirety of the season, lasting seemingly forever in a dried bouquet.

The young woman said it was the power of influence she wanted to explore. She wanted to investigate who had it, and how it worked. How did power propagate?

This was the start of many long conversations, and our classes often went over, but no one complained. We read both horticultural and literary texts and discussed them at length, writing reflections and responding to each other's ideas, and at the end of the term, we presented our finished work. I didn't present, myself, but I still say "we." It was an experiment in collaboration, in alchemizing ideas out of plants. It was meant to show how the history of human evolution arises from our literary relationship to the earth. The class was called "True Nature."

My beautiful student was last to present her work.

She said to think of a truth in nature is absurd. The birds, the flowers, the trees, the soil—each of these entities had a history that preceded its current state, and each stage of that history was informed by both regeneration and violence, and political and environmental factors that impacted it directly and indirectly. If there was any truth to be discovered, it was that nature itself was not neutral, and any so-called purity was imposed upon it by those of us with the need to use nature as a shield from our own complicity with systems of destruction.

It was impossible to simply "be" in nature, she said, without complicating the notion of "nature" itself, just as a border has nothing to do with the land's actual requirements for entry or exit. In fact, she said, it wasn't *nature* at all that man was searching for in his desire to exist closely within it, but a projection of the desire to be without politics, which man misinterpreted as being without consciousness. Man envied this seeming consciousnessless of nature, for he knew, deep down, that ego alone would never solve the problems of the heart.

But nature did have a consciousness, she said, or it *could* have one, or two, or twelve. It was that man had no way of knowing what form that consciousness took, or how to interpret it, let alone how to contain it or embody it, and he never would, unless he gave up all control forever, and not just the illusions of it.

She wrote this in the form of a play and performed all the parts herself as a surprise for me. Her idea was expressed through a reenactment of the funeral of Achilles from the perspective of the flowers growing near his funeral pyre.

It was exquisite.

And I was jealous.

I began to doubt whether her work was wholly original. There was something about her conceptual framework that felt familiar, established, as though it were something

I myself had studied. Of course, one could argue one's way in and out of anything, one could evoke feelings of ancient ideas and still be contemporary, and anyway, that was why we were here, it was the whole point of literature, to question, to interpret, and to reimagine.

I resisted the thought because I knew it was ungenerous, and yet it kept coming back in. I recalled her admissions essay to the course, which had been very good, but still, the sensation of wrongdoing ate at me. It just didn't seem possible.

I questioned her. You know, in the spirit of discourse.

It was the wrong thing to do.

She became a professor.

I've always been drawn to the written word. It began early on with comic books, and I read the same issues over and over. I never tired of battles between good and evil, stories of death and memory, all the darkness and all the light that felt so elusive to me then, so out of reach. I recall my mother relenting to my plea to please, let me read at the dinner table.

The more time passed, the more books I had to get through, and I began to read as if in a race against time. Simple pleasure in reading, the childhood delight of hunkering down with a good book and a warm bagel on my chest, sitting sideways on a sunken armchair with my head on its arm, no longer felt possible. Reading became an intellectual pursuit, one of focus instead of escape.

But maybe, with age, imagined realities that had felt out of reach and otherworldly began to feel more real, and this realness was what stripped the luxury out of the act of reading. The more I knew, the less I was moved by the fantastical stories I had reveled in as a child. Fables and allegories had once worked their magic on me, but now that I was capable of seeing how the tricks were done, and even able to play those tricks myself, I was bored. Now, when I read, nothing new occurred to me. Perhaps I had moved away from reading entirely, but the idea was frightening.

Was this what some people called analytic contentment?

I did not feel content. I wrote and read to get back to the ravenousness of childhood, to those days of dogeared comics stained with cream cheese at the corners.

But I also did it to prove that my mind was growing into something more than a child's.

I didn't think I had come to the end of my utility. I looked down on my younger colleagues with their notions of what education could accomplish. They wanted too much. They wanted to reinvent everyone's methods. They wanted to do away with the systems that they felt imprisoned them, and yet in a way, they enjoyed their imprisonment because it gave them something to abhor. I found them lazy. They hated working. They just argued and argued. I asked them to take walks with me through peaceful places in the city, and they refused. Why would we walk? They asked, when we could talk right here?

What did they want from me? To cease to exist?

There's such a thing as empathy, I told my colleagues. Don't forget to be *kind*, I said. Don't forget about joy! Whatever happened to having fun?

I had always been one of the outsiders, or so it had felt. I had led the way, written a map of alternative paths. And now they were asking me to kindly get out of the way. I guess I should have just done that, moved aside. But it's not so easy.

On the other side of my career was a threatening darkness. The darkness not of mystery but of fear.

Perhaps, I told myself, there was a way I could see it as a risky adventure in self. After years of being face-down in water, maybe now I had an opportunity to flip over, maybe I could publish new work—it had been so long—to correct the misinterpretations. I could rebut the critique of my beloved department, the diminishment of my value, by providing the public with a work that challenged my colleagues' precious positionality, the ethics of relying on identity for the cultivation of merit, work that was about nature in its *totality*. Something rooted in the land. I'd set out into the wilderness and write about my experiences training falcons, eating nothing but seeds and mushrooms. Now, finally, I had time. It would be a work of genius—as my writings had been referred to once before, but not lately. A word I liked to say demanded definition, yet how can one define magic? I was attached to it, that word. But I only used it with a sense of embarrassment.

There are books that move people just by being read, my colleagues said. Books that are *for people*. Then there are books that can only move people who come to those books with prior knowledge, who have read the other books to which this new book alludes. Such books, among which my colleagues included my own, could only be considered complete when they were reflected upon by scholars: the people responsible for writing and then reading the books to which books like my own made reference. These reflections, too, would then be couched in a language too confusing for most readers to understand. You had to be willing to work hard to learn it. You couldn't just read, you had to *have read*. To learn, you had to already know.

To my young colleagues, the best kinds of books—the ones that could move people just by being read—were like picnickers on the side of highways. There they were, sitting comfortably on the grass with a sandwich, wiping their hands on their pants, visited by deer and by sunlight.

Whereas my books were like clouds, up high, with matter but no mass.

I can appreciate the need for books that entertain, but I ask: Can *you* imagine contemplating a groundbreaking idea while eating a sandwich?

I do like sandwiches, of course.

I thought mostly about my career and making it better, especially when I was walking in the natural spaces that still existed in the city. It was in cemeteries, especially, where I found myself most overcome with worry: Had I done everything I could have? Would anyone remember me? I had no children.

My colleagues said I took few risks when it came to hiring, and they accused me of reacting to departmental changes with a subtle, quiet redirection, followed by a willful forgetting. I always told myself this deprioritization was because the institution at large was an unfriendly home to revolutionary ideas and their makers, not that I was unfriendly to them myself. But they felt otherwise.

I was not a bad man. Nowhere near it. But they said I was anyway.

They called me a taker.

It was natural, my colleague had said, to reject this thought, to consider myself a doer. She said most people identified as such. But a doer is someone who volunteers and makes sure a given job gets done. A taker, by contrast, is the person in the meeting who tries to seem invisible, who thinks, "How could they ask more of me, when I am already doing so much?" A taker thinks about how much they need, not about how their need's fulfillment might affect others. Whereas a doer is a person who takes positive action to benefit others.

A taker—me, she said—is someone who allows themselves to benefit from the *actions* of doers without making a contribution of their own. And, she said, no one really thinks, "I'm a taker," because this would mean acknowledging that they act largely in their own best interests. And even when someone does have a moment of doubt, worrying that they might be a taker, who would admit it? And certainly no one would *aspire* to be one. To hear people talk, every one of them is a doer, and all their ambitions are centered upon achieving greater feats of doing.

This is only logical, according to my colleague, who had her theory nicely buttoned up. Even if there were someone in the world who knew themselves to be a taker, who could *accept* that they were a taker? To make this admission would mean telling yourself and the world that your life had been spent exploiting the doers and the systems they had created to better *do* their *doing*.

To be an effective taker one must look like a doer.

It must be imperceptible.

My colleague said, of course, some people had every *right* to take. Some people had had so much taken *from* them—by takers, one assumes—that they had an *obligation* to tip the scales back toward balance. But that didn't mean they were takers. They were just taking, and there was a difference. A taker, by definition, is someone who already has enough, who could afford to share but will not. Takers cry out for redistribution of supplies while hiding extra food in their basements, stuffing their provisions under quilts. And if they eventually went back to their cellars to discover that all the food that they had sequestered was rotting, takers cleaned up the muck bemoaning their bad luck even though they must have known all along that to hoard the food was to risk its becoming useless.

A taker who thinks they are a doer spends a good deal of time suggesting ways for people not to be takers. A doer, on the other hand, is too busy to theorize.

I suppose she considered herself a doer, didn't she. Obviously.

Oh, it was tiring.

And it goes on!

Sometimes a taker who wishes they were a doer will occupy themselves with time-consuming tasks of no utility, tasks with no measurable result save using up time, no aim save to better convince themselves and their peers that they are a doer, like cutting wood for a furnace that uses only oil. A taker has to have an elevated sense of self, enough that they can't see the implications of all their taking, they have to see it as political, as meaningful. Whereas doers cannot have elevated senses of self. Doers just do, and then, on their days off, recover from doing.

Even worse, my colleague said, takers often judge doers for what little taking they have to do in order to survive, as if to take anything from life was to become, oneself, a taker, which of course, it isn't, because it all depends on what you need! These takers go around asking doers to be more generous and to join the cause of giving, because to give is more valuable and a higher calling than mere doing.

Takers who really think that they're doers are worse than takers who just take.

Better to just take and wallow in the taking like a hog.

Of course, it might be that no one was *solely* a taker or a doer through their lives. Probably people flopped back and forth. Were takers one day and doers the next. One could even imagine doers voluntarily joining a community of takers because it could seem to them that this would make them more efficient in their doing. From afar, takers do seem to be nothing if not efficient. And would the takers ever expel a doer from their ranks?

Not on your life.

This woman was sorting people. She was *sorting* them! And what was it but *taking* to waste my time with these endless categorizations? But I let her speak at me. I nodded agreeably.

The fact was that war had been declared against me. On one side there was me, and on the other a faction of women who delighted at the slightest hint of my vulnerability. They were hysterical, I thought, and maybe evil, words I could only bring myself to whisper in the closest confidence for I knew the politics behind their deployment.

I longed for someone to eradicate them.

But no one said a word. The very people I thought might rally to my cause, who had once idolized me, instead got down on their knees before my persecutors. I had no one on my side. Not even my wife who had to be seen to remain neutral. And yet she agreed with me—I knew she agreed.

I had been betrayed by a system that once valued mastery and now seemed only to value its redistribution. It wasn't fair, and it was dirty.

What about a moral code. A sense of decency! No true ally would have dared to stoop so low as to question the character of a man so kind, so plant-loving, so mild-mannered as I, suffering so much from being forced into the confines of these women's newly minted stereotypes of maleness, stereotypes that like all stereotypes sought to simplify, to reduce, reduce, reduce, like the theories of my colleagues, theories that were created to destroy, to dismantle and ridicule, as sheer exercises of power. Categorizations founded on rage, not research. Written with a violence that frightened me. With a disgust that disgusted me. My colleague talked about men, about me, about "us," and she ridiculed our position. And yet I was different. I was hardly a man in its modern sense, but a man in search of his true nature, in search of a pure and burbling spring far out in the dark wood.

It was a kind of game to her, this woman—when it was my life!

I grazed my wife's hair from her face. I tucked it behind her ear. I did this so she could see something in its completeness. Yes, it was a lovely face. I adored it before she betrayed me. I admired it often, the way it remained the same, the way it was always somehow different. She intrigued me.

I told her to see something for the first time is to see it in its completeness. Never again will the thing be seen anew. Never again will the rush of surprise associate itself with it. The first time is a revelation, and everything afterward is mere sameness. To find the complexity in sameness, however—that is art. This was something I tried to teach my students. It was something I tried to teach my wife.

I was delighted by her. Though she also repulsed me. When she was a student, and later when she became my wife. She annihilated me by knowing things I didn't know. My desire was something about her I could control, and ultimately, marrying her was the greatest revenge against her brilliance. When she was my student, deep down, I wanted to lick up and down the route between her breasts. But she *was* my student, and so I kept this desire sublimated, entirely. I tell you: entirely.

But, when she stopped being my student and became a professor—*years* later, many years—we found ourselves in a room together. She asked me would I be interested in reviewing a book by her friend. The subject of the book fell into my area of interest, or roughly anyway.

I said: Of course. I've been hoping to touch you.

I meant *talk to you*. But I said, "touch."

For *years*, her overpowering odor, the herbaceous smell of a seaside cliff, the moss. She was a pragmatist, she was granite and driftwood. She hated me so much, and it was a part of her, my desire for her, that I could control. I said the words I meant, although I didn't mean to say them, because I had yet to evolve. I was a man, obsessed with the shape of her body. But she was older then, so in a sense it had been predestined.

I knew men who had paid for sex, with money or with objects of value, exchanging something of theirs in return, and these men panted by the copiers outside the faculty lounge. The idea of these men had never taken up residence inside of me. And yet, I had taken the idea in without knowing. They panted, I had judged them for their panting, and now their panting was *in me*. I was those men. This is what I worried my colleagues thought about me, anyway, that I was *those men*. Simply because she had once been my student, long ago.

I was not those men.

I was nothing like those men.

We were only human! She approached me, or had I approached her? We had approached each other at a fundraising event. Our presence was mandatory, our work was being honored, she was now a professor, she had written a celebrated play—I pretended to have read it—and we were there in service of our institution. Her friends were there, our colleagues, but my former student who was now a professor—she wanted to talk to *me*.

I apologized to her. For questioning her those years back about the play she had written in my class. I made my sorry brief; I had learned that apologizing is often worse than saying nothing.

She didn't care. She thought it was funny. I was always funny, she said, from day one. And in fact, she wanted to talk somewhere else. She wanted to continue the conversation.

I was confused and elated, my hunger for her was overwhelming. Those years. All the years of wanting, of being destroyed. Because, her play, it was directed at me. It *felt* directed. It was pointed. It pointed right at me. And it was convincing to so many. But it was also misguided. It was laughable really, or it was almost laughable. She was laughing and she had been laughing! She knew. You know what I mean—it had lost its power. There had been a momentum behind it, but it wasn't as strong as the momentum against it. She had good ideas and she needed time to perfect them, time that I had spent already, time they couldn't take back from me. I was inspired by her and yet I also believed that I knew more than she did. It was a complicated feeling, to know more, but to be inspired.

We were at her house, upstairs, in a little closet without a door. Be quiet, she said. Her neighbor had children. The walls were thin.

I let myself go. She wanted me! I couldn't have cared less about her play, then. I told her I was like her dog, loyal, devout. I told her that, like her dog, I waited for her in the campus courtyard. I told her that, like her dog, I would lick her hello, I would lick her awake, I would bathe her, I would shelter her in my tongue's old house. I would chain myself up to the porch. I said all this while making love to her, my hands grabbing the meat of her hips. Shut up! I encouraged her, remembering the neighbor's children, and I gave her a slap because I liked the sound of her as much as the smell.

Afterward, she told me to get out.

The next week, we had lunch.

Later, we were married.

Later still, she left me.

They called me a "colonial artifact." I couldn't say anything in my own defense, or anything at all; the sight of my lips parting to form a sound inspired protest and rancor. My wife was part of these meetings and she remained silent. She couldn't really say anything, she said. She had to remain objective. These disagreements were between myself and other faculty. Between my ideas and theirs. They were personal, they were unique to my position and to myself as contrasted with the positions and selves of the women attacking me. How could she intercede?

We felt defeated. We were depressed. I say we, but no, it was me; she could not feel what I was feeling. She was friends with these women. She admired these women. And they admired her. But what was the good of their brilliant words, I asked, if they were meant to *eradicate*? Wasn't the world ugly and angry enough as it was?

I told my colleagues they were clever, I told them they were influential, so I encouraged them to influence for justice. They laughed at me. It was just another tactic, they said.

Again, no one defended me.

So, I tried my best to evolve.

I longed to be free from the criticism, to just exist. But when faced with the question of how to exist, the humiliation lay waiting. Who was I without my position? Where was I going? For a while it felt that all of it—everything in my life—might still return to normal someday. Surely the days when I was somebody, when I was adored, could not be gone for good. The dust of culture would settle, and I would emerge, stronger than ever, as if I'd only been away for a while, on a long vacation; I would emerge heroically from a propeller plane, back from the long journey of hunting big game in the great unknown. Perhaps the war was something I'd come to see as a gift—the gift of extra time, of extra space, in which to create something new, or to free myself from the chains of mediocrity. I held onto this hope as one might the sight of distant water in the desert. But it was a mirage.

My wife said she had given her life to supporting my vision. Her work had been sidelined for the sake of my work. I'm a hat stand, she said. Sidelined how, I asked her. Completely, she said. And she was done.

The dog officially took my spot on the bed. I moved into the guest room with the bad mattress. Not even the way we made coffee made sense anymore. There was only enough for one cup and a little extra, so we made coffee separately. She would go to dance class at night and I would pretend to be asleep when she got home. I would hear her greeting the dog with such happiness. Then the shower would go on. She didn't even think to look for me.

Then came the whispers, singing songs about unworthiness. They told me that the world would be better off without me. The thoughts were like knives in the head.

I would hear music filling silent rooms. The music was a reminder that I was still alive, yet I could not have heard it without the existence of a silence that contained nothing.

They said they were sorry. The department had to evolve. It wasn't fair, they agreed. But the truth in this case was relative or was beside the point. Either way, nothing was true. So, everything was. We're really doing you a favor, they said.

I guess I was relieved. But I was also sad.

Beware the storytellers, I told my students on my last day. They'll build you a world you'll prefer to your own.

I read that somewhere, a student said. She was right. I had written it.

Collecting unemployment would have been nice, although I saw that the social benefits of resigning far outweighed the economics of termination.

My wife and I tried to do something about the chasm between us. We saw a therapist. A pathetic waste of time. We went to a tantric sex workshop in Iceland. It was cold. Everything, my wife said, was about me finding pleasure. No, I said, everything was about the dog.

I began to swim. Which didn't help either.

I could take no more solace in observing nature because I no longer had any patience for losing myself in anything at all. What I wanted was enjoyment, but I did not know how to enjoy. And the city's green spaces now seemed grotesque. These places were not nature at all, but gestures, mere gestures.

I yearned for the real thing.

ACT 2

REALTOR

You were beloved, how could you not be. I can tell you're a great conversationalist; you ask open-ended questions that get people talking. They must have been inspired by you. I can imagine that someone like you suffered there. How can anyone have good ideas in a cesspool? You must have felt suffocated, or maybe it gave you good ideas? Either way, I can imagine you were sick of it, and I can imagine you were more than happy to go when they asked you to leave. I imagine you felt a relief, in the way that any situation which offers good pay is hard to leave behind, and then when you leave it there's this relief, as if they solved your problem for you. Their loss—you left and continued your illustrious career, and they couldn't take the credit anymore!

Helen left the city. Helen, the owner of this house. She left the city a long time ago and she never looked back. She came here and said it was the best decision she'd ever made. She wanted to get back to something elemental. And she found it. Right here, in this house!

She was like you. She had a sense of the *world*.

And, by the way, she was preoccupied with honesty. She had no patience for falsity of any kind. Not that she valued sincerity over everything else. In fact, she would sometimes say sincerity can also serve as a shield or screen for callousness; a good way to hide your hateful or selfish feelings. Often, she said, you'll see the least altruistic people using sincerity to throw their weight around. Honesty and sincerity are great ways to avoid suspicion, she would always say.

Helen could see through those honest people right away, just by the way they glanced at their reflections in the window behind her when they talked. The moment she would catch someone doing this Helen would give up on them. This might make her sound like a pretty intolerant person, but isn't it the other way around? Yes, *they* were intolerable. And Helen refused to abide by their fake humility. She preferred outright liars over the false-caring people. She'd rather spend time talking to a horrible person who was up front with their horribleness than someone trying their best to pretend they had nothing nasty lurking underneath.

You know what I mean...

She believed she was no worse and no better than most people and that we're all equally exceptional and equally doomed. But Helen had an optimistic view of the world. And you can tell as much by the house, by its energy. Because even though she feared the world's collapse, she also had faith in the systems of nature to rebound.

The realtor talked as she walked around the house. She paused every few minutes to let me take in details. I liked that she talked, and I was listening, but only with half of my attention. I was sick of talking, and I was tired of being wrong. I had been given the advice to listen more. I had been on a listening campaign, in a way. I knew that I had to listen or else I would have to speak up. And I had gotten good at listening. But did I hear? Yes, I heard. I heard, and I was listening.

Do you dream?

Because I used to have this recurring dream about being a typist. My job was to type up the notes and speeches of a very powerful man. I had this dream once a month, maybe. For years. Every day this man had to offer his words in a kind of newspaper that would be shared with the public. They were counting on his words, and he never missed a day. And neither did I, his typist, who slept in the office and stored all my personal effects in a locker behind the man's hat stand. I was a fast typist. I did shorthand and never looked down. I never made errors and the powerful man liked that because it meant he didn't have to worry. If he had worried, he would have lost his train of thought and that would have made him angry. So, he was happy because I never made mistakes and he would talk, sometimes for hours, riffing and theorizing on his subject of the day and I would type and the tapping of my typing became almost a rhythm and his speeches were like a melody, we were like a band.

I didn't listen to what the man *said*. I was so focused on the words themselves and the order in which he said them and trying to remember long strings of words, staying on top of his words and my typing, and not looking down so I could register the emotion on the man's face. I did not register the story he was telling or any details of any other kind, other than words stacked on top of words. After a few months—because who knows time, right, you're in a dream—the man seemed to get angrier and angrier and angrier. He would take longer and longer pauses and would reach down on his desk and pick up a tumbler glass and take sips from it and there would be full minutes of him just sitting there, him silent and me waiting for him to start saying something again. I wanted to be half a step ahead of him, to anticipate the word he was going to say so that I could be writing the end of the word just as he began speaking it.

I guess you could say I got to know him and how he thought, even though I wasn't really aware of the things he was saying. The content of them, I mean.

But the more he paused and the more he paced around the room the more I could actually listen to the words. And the words were terrible! Words about madness and pain, words that were unkind and merciless. The more he paused the more I listened and the more I hated myself for what I was typing, the more I hated the words coming out of my fingers and the more I wanted to just stop typing and throw it all away and get up and walk out. But I needed the money. This was a dream and yet, I still needed money, isn't that funny? I needed it so much that I couldn't stop typing because no one was hiring typists like me, there was no one like him who made so many speeches who refused to type their own speeches. I needed this job, but I couldn't bear to type the words he was saying. He didn't reread the speeches after I typed them. He said he had no time to look back. What he said was momentary, he told me, and if he read it later, he would be missing out on the moment he was currently in. The now.

I began to alter his speeches just the slightest bit when I was typing. Just the smallest bit! So that someone who noticed my tiny changes in tone might have thought the man was only kidding. Little by little I altered what I typed from what the man was saying and began to hate myself less, and eventually I even began to enjoy myself. It was risky, but no one noticed. They were such small things, insignificant tense changes or pronouns that might just have been a lesser typist's error but in my case was an art unto itself.

One day the man received a phone call from a reporter who wanted him to comment on one of his statements, one of the statements I had subtly altered. I was in the room with the man, typing—even though I was dreaming—and I thought to myself—in the dream!—this is the end. But the man just laughed into the receiver. "Comment?" the man said, "Ha! I only live in the now," he said, "I never dwell on the past." And he hung up on the reporter without even asking what the reporter wanted him to comment on.

I went on typing for another year, in my dream. One time I hid a code in a speech that gave out directions to a secret location where I wanted to meet a friend for drinks. When she found me there, sitting by the bar, we laughed harder than I've ever laughed, in a dream or in real life. On another occasion when the man wanted me to type up a cake recipe from his grandmother, I put in the wrong measurements for the flour and the butter and sugar. Go ahead and make this cake, I dared his readership, who I held in great disdain because of their views of the world and their views of humanity. Go ahead and choke on it and die!

I haven't had the dream in years, but I think about it often, so it's nearly a memory at this point.

I told her it was an interesting dream. Then I asked her if I could step outside for a moment and have a cigarette on the deck.

So, you're a smoker! I'm going to be honest, I guessed it when you walked in. I should get you some of the herbal cigarettes Helen used to smoke. She used to store them in the broom closet.

Poor Helen, in assisted living. Can you imagine? Living with assistance after having lived without assistance for so long in this beautiful house? She made that sculpture, over there in the corner. Imagine being so deft with a chainsaw, building that massive sculpture, smoothing it with your own hands, and then spending your life in constant need of assistance. She asked me many times, help me die. Don't put me in assisted living! Everyone asks, why is she selling? And I say, she's gone to live with her son, she's too old for this place. But I'll be honest with you, she doesn't have children.

Anyway, smoke. Smoke.

Just keep the door shut so the smell doesn't come in.

Breeze, air, trees, the sky. Birds and sounds. Shadows and hillsides. We were way out there.

I wasn't a smoker, but I was smoking. It was all part of the darkness I was in. The smoking, the terrible way it made me feel.

I came back in. I told her it was nice to be in the country, where nature could really express herself.

Yes, it's beautiful. People thinking about moving to the country think, how could I ever leave the city, there couldn't possibly be life outside of the city. But I always laugh at that. Anyone who thinks "how could I ever leave the city" is not meant to live here in this beauty, that's the end of the story. I left the city. Helen left the city. But I'll tell you the truth, everyone who comes to look at this house doesn't *actually* want to leave the city. They want to buy the house and let it rot, they want it as a Plan B in case the world ends. They want to let the weeds choke out the poppies. But these poppies have been here for eighty years. Helen's aunt planted these poppies, *Papaver orientale*, she tended them for so long and then some person who doesn't want to leave the city is going to buy this house as a contingency plan, let the house rot, let the poppies get choked out, and come, what, once a year, twice a year? It's a tragedy is what it is. Helen in assisted living, and this incredible house rotting.

This is a place you could plant a beautiful garden. A place where you could live bucolically. Is that a word, "bucolically"? I bet you're thinking, I'm a lucky man. Well, you *should* be thinking that, because you're the last person I'm showing this house to, and then I'm taking it off the market. I've decided it's too good to sell. You're lucky to see it, before I take it off.

This is a house that could be in magazines. In fact, it was once. It was in a magazine, a piece about the renovation. Helen fixed it up, years back. It's around here somewhere, in a binder.

We went out on the deck. There were just fields and rolling hills. I offered her a cigarette. She laughed. She accepted and then smoked while she talked.

There used to be a lot of farms around here. Now you see empty silos and old houses, you saw them on your drive in. But agriculture here used to be more natural and diversified, a system of family farms, one after another. This house is amazing because you can only see the fields and the hills, no houses, and it's that kind of view that's closest to paradise, don't you think?

I did think it was like paradise. Still, I told her she was likely overselling it. She laughed at that. And yet I said I also thought it was as good as it seemed. She laughed at that, too.

Way back when, farming families around here had their own vegetable gardens and knew how to raise their own livestock for meat, and women made jam and bread and they didn't rely on imports. People knew how to take care of themselves, is what I'm saying, they knew how to survive in a world that was edging them out. If you meet an old man who has missing fingertips, you can bet he was a farmer! That sort of thing happened from time to time.

But they were farming for *real*, professor. They weren't *gentlemen* farmers. People who farm for fun say "farming" but it means something very different from the farmers who couldn't say anything *but* farming.

I told her this was something I had taught my students, that definitions differ depending on who says the word.

I read that you were a teacher. I read about you a bit, actually. You taught the transcendentalists. I always thought they were a bunch of evangelicals, by the sound of it. But they believed in the divinity of *nature*, of course. I learned that later!

But let me teach *you* a little something. Did you know that after the war, the government had an excess of chemicals left over from making bombs? Did you know that after the war, they made an arrangement to increase the value of the raw chemicals, make some money off them? These are the sad truths of the world, professor. The government sold the chemicals to the farmers. As if the farmers had any use for chemicals. They worked the soil, back then. They used manure. It was simple back then. Small.

Sure, yeah, they gave farmers a great deal on a magic potion that would increase their yield while reducing the work done by men, and, by the way, at that time these were men who were in high demand. Replace man with machine, there we go. Drench the fields with a chemical to make crops grow faster and get bigger, then use a chemical to keep the weeds and bugs at bay. Just buy these chemicals and you'll see, you'll never have to work again! And that sounded good, didn't it, because no one liked working all that much, or no one wanted to work more than they had to.

And look at you, you're smoking the same chemicals, the same ones, professor, and you think you need it, too.

The first year it went well. All the pests died, and the crops were plentiful. So, there was growth. This is how they get you, at first, with *growth*. The family farms grew and consolidated, and the farmers became dependent on the potions, but they were happy to be dependent. It felt like being taken care of, a country that was taking care of its people who had been through so much. But soon, the farmers couldn't farm without the potions, because without the potions there were too many pests and no way to get rid of them, and without the potions the soil was useless, because the soil had become dependent, too.

Farmers who had been making money then went into debt paying for the treated seeds and gallons and gallons of the inputs, boxes and boxes, whole vats of it, which had originally been sold as a miracle cure, but now were being sold as the solution to what was seen as continual disease. The companies were making new potions to answer the problems that had been created by the old potions, and the farmers bought the new potions, and the companies blamed the farmers for bad practices or bad soil or bad weather or bad work ethic. They had to work harder now, but it was all about dousing their soil, you see, the work had become all about dousing the soil and forgetting about what made the soil itself in the first place.

It was an endless parade of potions, professor. And farms were buying up other farms and there was monocropping and no one grew their own kitchen gardens anymore, everyone was reliant on selling one crop for acres and acres, all the way up to their dooryard. Subsidies were granted by the government to help farmers afford even more magic tricks. The livestock got sick from eating grain because of the chemicals in the grain eating away at their gut. "But cows get sick," said the companies, and they gave the cows medicine that was made by the industry that had extra antibiotics it needed to sell, which were made from some of the same chemicals. "Just give the cows this medicine," the companies said, and the animals took the medicine and became resistant to it and got sick again and took more, higher doses, new compounds made by those companies, or by their sister companies.

Helen and I used to discuss this right here, this stuff about *the world*, right here on the deck, and right in there on the built-in couch. We used to sit here when it was nice and drink whiskey, otherwise we'd sit in there and drink wine, and she'd smoke an herbal cigarette and, I'm not going to lie, sometimes I'd smoke one, too. We would discuss farming and the world. We would say, aliens must be studying us, because there can be no other reason we're all still alive. Helen would say, humans are horrific but we can also be empathetic, and aliens are studying us because of our ability to love alongside our tendency to torture each other. Helen would pull out her knife and whittle, and there'd be little sparks of woodchips flying around. She'd throw her knife at a log by the fire to store it. That thing would fly by my head just about, sticking in the wood like a dart.

Helen, in assisted living. And this house, just sitting here, empty. It's terrible, this work of art. Houses can get lonely too, you know.

But here's the thing. I ask you, professor, *who* was in charge of looking into theories and *who* was in charge of creating studies for how the chemicals had taken over the world and what could be done to save farming? The land grant universities is who, the ones the farmers had once relied on for soil analysis! The *universities* were going to solve the problem. But the problem was that the *universities* had replaced the soil scientists who knew the real benefits of soil with scientists from the chemical companies, and money was funneled into research and studies of yet more chemicals to fix the problems that had been started by the chemicals in the first place. The studies were skewed and quantitative analysis of the state of agriculture was skewed because it relied on the skewed data. Knowledge about soil and crops came from the thinkers at the land grant universities who were put in place by the chemical scientists who advised the companies to continue putting time and money into creating more inputs for the crops that now couldn't survive without them.

It's not that I'm against the universities, but I just think we need to ask ourselves more often, what good are they?

I told her I didn't think they were any good at all.

They're not better than starlings, that's for sure. Nothing could be as beautiful as a murmuration of starlings, which looks like smoke come to life. I'll bet you nothing at a university could be that beautiful. You might know a thing or two about birds, professor, but there's no way you know what a murmuration *feels like*.

It's amazing, you know, because they don't collide.

They're better than the universities, professor, better than all those buildings and all those ideas. But the thing is, a murmuration looks like the plague, too, coming for you. They look like locusts, but it's so *beautiful*, like this proof of wild things having an intelligence far greater than ours. The way they move, like a swarm of bees.

You know what I mean, like traffic. Have you ever driven in traffic and thought to yourself, it's a miracle there aren't more accidents? I think about that every time I'm in traffic. I think about it when I'm driving and another car comes at me from the other direction, and we pass each other and we're a foot apart, separated by one line. It's the most natural thing in the world, hurtling past each other the way we do, it's beautiful chaos, and most of the time we are okay.

Then sometimes we do collide. But starlings never collide.

They must collide, I thought. They must have collided at least once. I was listening, remember. I was listening carefully. And I was happy to be listening, even if I thought she might be wrong.

More importantly, what happened to the *soil*, professor? Rains came, and the soil was washed away into rivers. The water became toxic. Winds came, and the air became toxic. Farmers lost money and were faced with no other option than to accept handouts from the government who relied on the chemical companies for funding.

It's a *joke*. This country. The farmers got sick, and their kids got sick, and they had to take medicine that was made with chemicals, too, just like the livestock, only these treatments were designed to kill all the cells in order to get at the bad cells, so there weren't many good cells left. And I ask you, where did the science for the medicine come from? Yep, you guessed it. The universities!

Everyone was being edged out by someone else. The cities were getting more and more crowded, and the farmers who weren't growing any food for their families had to continue buying cheaper and cheaper food that was made with the chemicals and the crops they had, at least in part, grown on their fields but could not eat. Fewer and fewer people could remember the days when they grew their own vegetables and milked their own cows and it all became a fable, people talked about homesteading, but they also forgot about who fished in the rivers before the homesteaders. No one's memory could go that far back. Memory was being eaten up. Memory was being erased!

Grandparents would say "back in my day," but no one really believed them, and anyway everyone was looking toward the future. Some farmers who could see they were being tricked tried to pull themselves out, but they were met with a monstrous force of legal power that threatened their lives and they were harassed. Bankruptcy, suicide, and the seeds they had didn't even reproduce—if you tried to save seeds you would be thrown in jail. Birds and bees were sick, livestock were knee deep in shit and despair. People ate the despairing meat and became despairing, too, and the companies, the land grant universities, the government's response was *more*.

And now I've depressed you.

I told her I was already depressed.

You could have the bucolic life, here, though, on this land, if you worked for it. The real kind of bucolic. The kind of breezy summer days that people only distantly remember nowadays. Helen and I used to sit right here and talk about how breezy this life was, perfect, peaceful, apart from time.

I liked the idea, I told her, of that kind of life. She made it sound easy, I told her, but I knew it must be difficult.

It *is* difficult. But in an easy kind of way. I mean, it's the kind of difficult you have some say over.

It's curious that you should be interested in this life alongside those big ideas of yours. I've never read your work, but I looked you up, just a little. I know the media just wants to sell an ad, so I didn't read too deep or too far into things. We all need to leave old lives because we outgrow them, is what you said. "We all need to experience ourselves anew." You wrote about the idea of new starts. You wrote about the idea of being reborn. I read that piece of yours, the idea of helping others to give birth to something. I guess it's not true that I haven't read your work. Sometimes reading is pointless, though, and it's better just to take things in. You learn a lot by just looking and seeing.

It was a relief to just experience, I said, as opposed to reflecting on experiencing.

Yep, the emptiness of experience. An emptiness that isn't exactly empty.

This *house* is empty, for example, and yet the built-in couch makes it seem full, don't you think? Helen would lean back on this very built-in couch and hold a jar of wine and laugh. She would be telling me all her ideas, these deep philosophies, laying on her built-in couch, like the Greeks. You can joke about things, but we all know there's truth in jokes, and it's true, she fancied herself a little like the Greeks. But everyone who's looked at the house says, "How easy would it be to remove the built-in couch?" But it's the couch that holds the story! People are so *typical*.

Furniture holds energy, you know. Information. Memories. Every time you read something, like, "they sat at the dining room table," you think about a dining room table from your childhood. You hear about "chairs" and you think about the chairs from your childhood.

Well, Helen *made* furniture. And she used to say she was making memories. She said she wanted people to think of *her* chairs when they heard the word "chair" and that this would be the most important thing she could do, to build memories out of wood. But you know, she never had a mirror in the house. Mirrors were not *furniture*. People would ask Helen to design them a mirror and she'd refuse to work with them, she'd say no one should be looking at themselves, that looking at yourself in a mirror made it so you couldn't remember. You had to look at chairs and at tables, and *then* you would remember, but a mirror made you forget. Inside every person is a landscape, Helen would say. Why look at your reflection in search of the truth? We are more than just our puny selves, and mirrors are all about puniness. All the mistakes we may have made, these are mistakes that come from looking too hard at our reflections. If we had no reflections, we'd see what was in front of us, we'd see many things at once, none of them ourselves. Helen would say we should look for a reality beyond the self where we can see things as a collective entity. A community. This is something to strive for, a life that plays within that entity.

I said this to my colleagues, many times, I told the realtor. I had used the word "community."

But it's about the words around the words, professor. It's even *more* about the words around the words, than the words themselves.

Now that I think of it, maybe Helen meant that it was not the things that stared back in the mirror but the things within the core of one's *teaching* which stared back. That the *teaching* was what was reflected in our faces, and we could not escape what we had been taught. It's not easy to transfer knowledge, and it's not easy to get rid of it, either. To teach is one of life's most complex gestures, and its most humane.

Helen used to say that teachers were saints, because all day they had to deal with other people's children. Most teachers were teachers their whole lives, and while few started as a teacher and became something else, plenty of people started as something else and became teachers later. Once you were a teacher, you became a saint, because you'd chosen to commit to the world's children, she would say. You had the most important job in the world, helping raise up young people and teaching them how to read and how to be themselves and how to follow rules, and even if the rules were monstrous, a teacher taught about how to create better, more rational rules. But of course, there are bad teachers.

I sound like a child, don't I? Talking about truth and lies, about good and bad teachers.

You must be hungry. Here, have an apple. When you're done, just open the door and hurl the core off the deck. The deer will thank you for it. Isn't that freedom, hurling your core off the deck so a deer can eat it, then coming back in and sitting on your handmade, built-in couch? Have two, please, help yourself, that's why they're here.

I took an apple.

I heard on the radio today about a group of apple pickers who got sick with a mysterious illness. The workers were living in a cramped bunkhouse and because of their sickness had left the orchard without pickers. That's why the apple you're holding is more expensive than usual. I bought the apples without thinking, and now, maybe it's all the talking about Helen, now I'm wondering if I should have done more than just *buy* the apples. You know what I mean, weighing the choices? I could have reached out to the orchard, inquiring about the safety of their workers.

Helen would say, you could have gone out and harvested

apples yourself from your *own* orchard. But the fact is, it's past apple season in this orchard, but in the orchard where these came from, it's apple season.

I bet you've always wanted an apple tree, professor. Look at you, with that nice wool vest. You look like a man who needs an apple tree all his own. Well, here, during apple season, there are so many apples, you won't know what to do with them. But it's nothing compared to the birds. It's like a rainforest, professor. Birds all day.

Did you know there are desert birds who make communal homes that weigh up to a ton, that are twenty feet wide and ten feet tall? Like bird apartments, designed like human huts, with grass roofs that shed the rain, professor. Social weavers. They couple up and take care of their apartments. Don't you love the idea of birds coupling up and being like, "Where should we put the little nest for the baby?"

I lived like a social weaver before I moved here. Helen lived like a social weaver, too. In apartments, in the city. Stacked on top of each other, braving the elements, lining our nests with down and hoping for the best. We didn't know each other in the city, but we became close here.

And I don't miss the city a lick.

Not a lick!

Helen used to say that she didn't give a *lick* about anything. She used to say "you bet" instead of "you're welcome." Everyone up here says "you bet!" when you thank them for holding the door open.

Well, not everyone.

Everything here feels like Eden. Forget the city. You're probably thinking I'd say this about any house, but I sold a real dump last week and it didn't feel anything like this. I wasn't selling something I would *buy*. You know what I mean? I wasn't selling something I would live in. And I've lived in this house. I'm not the owner, but I've lived in this house as a close friend of Helen's for ten years. Ten years! This is Helen's house, but I lived here with her, as a close friend. I came here as a young woman. She took care of me, you could say, she taught me how to live. She taught me how to build a fire.

Yes, sir, this is my built-in couch as much as it's Helen's couch. She gave me the power to do what I thought was best, now that she can't do anything. Helen said, "Sell it if you want to, it's what you do." She went to assisted living because she couldn't even lift a cast-iron pan. I tried to take care of her, but she hated the sight of me in the end. The other week I went to visit her, but she had taken me off the visitor list. They wouldn't let me in. She has no next of kin and I am unable to assist her. And my mother back home is also in need of assistance. She's alone, Helen's alone. Everyone needs assistance. So, I told myself, just sell the house. I'll go back to my mother.

Listen, do you swim?

You can't see it from the house, but it's a short walk through the woods down the hillside over there. It's the best pond in the village, known for having the deepest and clearest water. It's shady and private, there's wild iris on the edge, a dock that stretches out for jumping, you couldn't ask for better. Swimming is true freedom, don't you think? There's nothing better than jumping into cold water on a hot day.

Cold water on a hot day, professor. That's freedom alright.

I bet you don't want to talk about your work. But I have to say it. Just humor me, just this once! I read your story about the egg hunt. It's not true I haven't read anything of yours, I did read "The Egg Hunt." Boy, did they misread that one! I had a whole theory about the roots of that story, and I talked about it with Helen. I read a bunch of essays about the story, there were so many things written about it, about all the ways it was *dangerous*, the way it *threatened* the birds. They thought it was dangerous!

Isn't it a joke, how you can tell a story and other people hear a different story than the one you told? What did they think, *you* had actually done that thing with the egg in your story? That it was about what *you did with the egg* rather than the idea of birds, of religion, about *Easter* and everything it brings up? I read it as religious. I thought it was well done. I love Easter. Boy, do I love Easter.

My mother took great pains to decorate our Easter eggs growing up. You could have written this into your story about the egg hunt, if you had known it, that my mother strung the eggs with sewing thread and arranged them on tree branches she had set in a large vase. But I bet people would say if you wrote that: "He's stringing them up! He's stringing them up! A pig, stringing them up, stringing up the eggs that stand for all of humanity, he's nothing but a sociopath, we should string *him* up!"

How can you even stand it? The media. The way they ridicule artists even though they need artists to exist.

I told her they needed artists as much as artists needed them.

And I read the story where you described your childhood. You managed to capture the feeling of religious desire in that one scene of the boy's communion, and the readers didn't get it, but why would they? Radical ideas are always rejected before they're recognized. You *have* to reject something if you're afraid of it. And they were afraid! They still are. I read all the essays about that story, too. Those people read it all wrong.

Now, I know exactly what you're going to say next. You're going to say it was a story and you weren't writing about *your* childhood, but childhood as a metaphor for something else. I hate it when artists pretend they're not writing about themselves when it's so obvious they are. What do you think? That we're stupid? That we care about *your* childhood? We only care about our *own* childhoods, so the work only means something to us if it reminds us of *our* childhoods. We read a book and sure, we'll deflect and talk about your childhood, but only so we forget that ours was so bad and hard, but really, we're thinking about our own childhoods the whole time. It's the critics who want to pretend they didn't have childhoods. That they are post-childhood. But we're all just children.

And what I read about your wife—wow, professor! Sounds like she's post-childhood, too. She's nothing but a hummingbird, if you don't mind my saying so. And you're nothing but a sapsucker, I'll be honest with you.

You ever seen a sapsucker, professor? They're like a woodpecker, but they suck the sap out of *living* trees, and peck away like a drummer in a marching band. They suck the sap out of live trees, and they paint these polka dots on the bark, they're peck wounds, and they suck the tree blood out until the tree dies. The holes look like bullet holes. Murderous little bastards. And get this, hummingbirds will time their migration and follow the sapsucker, just to get in on some of the action. Everyone thinks hummingbirds are so innocent, so small and ruby-throated, pulsing necks like dainty Victorians. Well, they're just as bad as sapsuckers, don't you think?

You almost have to feel bad for the hummingbird, in a way, because it's so small.

But the hummingbird is technically killing the tree, too.

Anyway, we're all just birds!

Helen used to make paintings on birch bark with sapsucker holes that she found in the woods. She'd paint them and hang them on outside of the barn, draping one of the holes over a nail. There are some still there, weathered and faded.

She learned how to paint when she was growing up, in the city. She grew up with a lot of money, can't you tell? She was a sapsucker, for *sure*. She had a lot of money to spend on this house, and a lot of money to lean on in hard times. I'm not mad, though, because she gave away money, too. She paid for my real estate license, for example, and she paid for a lot of other things.

You want to know that someone with money owned the house you're buying. It might sound tacky but it's just a fact. Someone with money won't cut corners.

I'm not supposed to say that, you know, *it's in the business handbook*, but I like you.

Helen had money. You betcha.

She used to say her life was like the inside of a golden egg, and that people with normal shells wanted nothing more than to be golden. And instead of thinking about their yolks or whites, they thought only of their shells and how they were missing some kind of decoration, whereas she had the decoration and wanted it to be normal, like theirs.

Helen was a golden egg who wanted to be *plain*. And yet she knew she was just an egg like every other egg, who only cared about her shell. She decided it was inside the shell that mattered. She decided to live her life according to the inside, not the outside.

Helen came to the country on a morning in early spring. She left the city and never went back. Never once! At first she lived with two other hippies who taught her how to hold an axe. She rejected all the trappings: electric heat, gas stoves, she slept under piles of blankets and knelt by the fireplace. This was a different house back then, an old farmhouse, the same structure but a different energy. It was before she put those many years of love and care into it.

They lost track of time as it had been. Helen and her friends measured accumulation in rows of jars. A good day's stock surge was the height and stability of a woodpile. They grew the beets, peeled them, then steamed them right up. They learned no amount of washing cleaned a T-shirt back to white, so they boiled up beet water and used it for dye. In the beginning they failed a lot, but when they discovered all the necessary mordants, they became affixed to their own independence. You like that? You would, you came up with it. "Affixed to their own independence."

What do you think, professor? Would you let me into your class? I bet you had some brilliant students. I read about you, and I read about your brilliant students.

I was surprised how much she knew about me, but then again, everyone knows everything nowadays. I was happy to discuss my work with someone who seemed to understand that life is complicated, someone who did their research. I trusted her, even though I knew she was selling me something.

Years went by, professor. More people joined in, and Helen said it was like a party all the time, but a party where you had to work. There were large gatherings and Helen recognized some other golden eggs who also wanted to be plain. There were lazy ones, too, who slept late into the day, swinging in a hammock between two trees while the workers were already hoeing weedy onions.

They shat in a bucket, professor, sprinkling on sawdust to absorb the smell. There were kettles of stew. They pumped the water right from the well, leaving buckets by the door with food scraps for the pigs. Sourdough heaved in a jar by the stove, and vines wound around the garden gate. A man with a beard and his sparrow pecked in the nasturtiums.

It sounds good right? What do you think, professor, idyllic?

How about this: Spoon carving with a well-honed knife, building a good stone wall that stayed still when you kicked it. A hot tub that's just a galvanized water tank on top of an open flame with little cedar slabs to sit on. Dogs without collars, cats in the henhouse. Bathing in the daytime, figuring out the borrowed cement mixer. A bandana on her head, a loom in the corner. Bags of wool, spinning wheels, raspberries by the back door.

They dreamed of a kind of technology that could take kids' old toys and melt them down into new ones. They avoided newspapers and some of them worked on future plans but were careful not to speak of them too loudly. It was a bubble, not a shell. It was more pliant. It could expand...

It was a dream the realtor was weaving. I felt a bit stoned on her descriptions.

Helen built outbuildings. Rotated pasture, fenced and stacked, dug and buried, planted and weeded, watered and harvested, and when she was done, she started over. She barely left her land except to get groceries and gas.

She covered her garden with fabric in fall and she didn't come in except for a storm, and only if there was lightening to go with it. As the hikers reached their peaks, Helen worked down below. And while she didn't see exactly from the height of a mountain, she still looked down on the world as if she were on some sort of summit.

It was about regeneration, Helen would say.

Do you believe in regeneration, professor?

I told her yes. At least I wanted to.

It's amazing to me that you've written so much and lived so fully, she said, and you're only fifty-one. Fifty-four? Fifty-eight? You don't look a day over forty-five.

Helen said she'd rather die than spend the rest of her days in assisted living. You couldn't possibly think that the rest of your life wasn't worth living at age fifty-four. You've written about so many things, but when you think about it, everything you've written has only been about life up to age fifty-four!

Forget about "the end." This is the beginning for you. I say you have a whole lifetime ahead of you. We don't even know what's out there. We're both young, in the scheme of things. You've left the city and maybe you'll never go back, but there's a whole life outside of the city! I can sell a house and I can throw in some idealism, too, can't I? Or are you a materialist?

You know, selling a house is very intimate. It leaves you vulnerable, thinking and talking about homes and lives and new beginnings. The buyer is always trying to prove their worth, hopeful that the seller will choose them over another buyer. Did you put any thought into me finding value in you?

I told her no, but I was lying.

I'll let you in on a secret. Buyers who want to buy hope the seller will think they're more virtuous than the other prospective buyers. Buyers tell sellers about all the things they believe in to prove they are most *invested* in the details of the listing. They want you to know they've done their research, that they've read all the fine print. But sellers are trained to welcome this enthusiasm even if it is repellant and predictable. Worse, the dreams which buyers so eloquently relay—including the dreams or fears of their partners—sound a lot like our own, even though we're not the ones buying. Of course, these visions from buyers are the products of the fantasy us sellers weave in the first place with our descriptions, the details we choose to disclose, the details we leave out on purpose.

I was taught that the best realtors inhabit the spirit of the house they are selling. They have to be able to see their world through the owner's eyes, every creak in the stairwell, every quirk of the kitchen, the way the front door sticks in the heat. And when they master a house, it becomes not just a listing, but a treasure to be discovered, a kind of beautiful, unpolished memory the buyer can build from.

It's sensual, in a way, because you're embodying the senses.

You're considered a master of your craft, right? That's what they wrote about you, those exact words: "A master of his craft." Well, guess what, I'm a master of my craft, too. Water damage on the north side of the building? A rusted roof? Exposed electrical wires in the guest room? A deck railing that isn't to code? The smell of mildew in the basement? Water that tastes sulfuric? The energy of a bad divorce? Maybe the floors are stained. Maybe there's rot in the corner of a low window where the snow piles up, soaking the insulation from the outside in. I would have been a great house inspector, but they only see the most obvious things, and I, on the other hand, know how to hide those things easily.

Me, I'm interested in details. Like how in spring, you can hear the peepers. They make a loud and glorious sound. It's the time of year you start to keep your bedroom windows open, you hear the breeze, a coyote in the distance, and the peepers...

I had lost track of time, but I had nowhere to be. It had gotten dark. There were no stars. The realtor was interesting, alternative, unkempt but colorful. She was odd, and she talked a lot. She was beautiful, I thought.

I can tell you really want to smoke again. Come on, let's have another. We can watch the storm roll in. Helen and I used to always sit out here and watch the storm clouds shoot off down the valley. They say it's going to snow tonight. This early in the fall, can you believe it? Give me my own, will you, I won't smoke the whole thing. I don't want to get back into it. But it's so tempting, smoking with you. It reminds me of my mother, same purple hands and cold cigarette.

When I got your email I thought, let me look into this fellow. But in real estate, we're told to pretend not to know who it is we're talking to. But what's the point, I do my research, everyone's on the internet.

There must be pressure, among your peers, to outdo each other, am I wrong? A tally, I'd imagine, for who has won what prizes. But here it's just hunting season, just gossip at the weigh station when you log the size of your buck. There's no internet for that. And there's no internet at this house, professor! No internet—isn't that amazing? Trust me, you don't want the internet.

You'd have to stay inspired to want to keep going in your line of work, I'd imagine. To feel there is room for you to make a difference. You'd have to acknowledge that some people are geniuses, and some people are there to waste your time, you'd have to decide which one you were or which one you wanted to be. I don't want anyone wasting my time, that's for sure, which is why I'm taking this house off the market. It's too beautiful! I couldn't bear the thought of selling this house to someone who didn't understand the root of everything we did here to make life *work*. The garden, the wood, the snow on the doorstep.

Don't try to stop me! Just kidding, professor. But seriously, I'm taking it off the market. I'm done trying to sell something that doesn't need selling.

Helen would hear of her friends from college who were protesting the war, who were participating in walkouts and while she empathized and supported the voices they were amplifying, she saw only the barriers to widespread change. She saw the roots. And they were looking at the leaves. Helen turned to her plot of land and the wisdom of the seasons. And she turned away from change, at least in that way.

But change is God, you know. I keep telling people, "Turn to the land, to the wisdom of the seasons," really, I say that, I say that all the time, but they don't care about the land or the seasons, they just care about the end of the world and having a place to hide out when the city doesn't feel safe anymore. But Helen, she felt purposeful and powerful being able to make her mark on the world in such a way that could be instantly visible, if only to her—a black square of soil punctuated by bright tufts of young, green lettuces; the pile of crescent-shaped horse-hoof trimmings on the stall floor; spears of garlic plants emerging from calf-deep mulch after the last snow melts.

Survive, professor! That's all you really have to do. Keep the grass from creeping into the carrots, deal with the woodchuck stealing the apples, patch up the pipes!

Helen's pants took a beating, her hands were chapped, her crow's feet deepened with the sun. You might be thinking it was a grand display of self-satisfied conceit, but she was filled with satisfaction. She knew she was working not just for herself but also for the bees. She walked behind her horses saying "come-gee, come-haw." She left pumpkins and potatoes in a makeshift farm stand at the bottom of her driveway with an old yogurt container for cash paid on the honor system. She let her hens go broody and she sold eggs, bought a Jersey heifer and was up with the cow at dawn, too, stripping away at her teats on the third leg of a parlor stool, bringing mason jars of milk down in coolers over ice, selling milk, selling cheese.

We used to talk about that kind of life, the beauty of it, the work, but professor, I'll be honest, it was *tiring*. I'm tired just talking about it. It's beautiful and it's also *tiring*.

But Helen seemed to never get tired, although she did say she felt inadequate compared to the wild animals who lived in the woods that surrounded her. They had no need for social contracts, they were living by an otherworldly governance that Helen could see but could not emulate. No amount of digging in the reeds and muck could make her completely forget the utterly frail, human world she belonged to.

Yes, professor, she became entirely separate from her generation as if she were living in a different time. She had visitors, but they were fleeing human frailty, too, and so they brought no news because they, too, were seeking to escape it.

She fell asleep early, exhausted just to have had the sun alive on her face for a time. And then, she got up early to sit on the deck with coffee to watch the fog lift, feel the dew suck back up into the air revealing the green daylight beneath it. To pay attention, you had to spend hours. To see the flight pattern of a bee, you had to sit idly beside a flower.

As an act of resistance against the world of corruptible ideas and false gods, Helen rejected all notion of their existence, refusing to engage in even a memory of the parts of her life that at one point held her attention. She didn't read, didn't go to the movies, didn't listen to music other than the classical station on public radio and, even then, should the host begin a commentary on the reputation of the composer and the mark they made on music's history, she would grab for the dial and switch it off.

Helen came to know a different kind of language, a different kind of art. She came to see that there are people who live completely apart from the minds that supposedly trigger seismic shifts in human history. There's contentment outside of all that, a life that sees no use for it. There are people who don't feel excluded, who aren't humiliated by their station in life, who don't compare themselves to those who may be seen as better, bigger.

There's more than one world on this Earth. And when Helen laid face-down in the garden and watched what mattered most on the top six inches of it, Helen saw a web of life, language, history, and tension that consumed her completely and had nothing to do with the life, tension, and history of what had come before.

In the fullness of time she became more accustomed to the words of natural systems. She became more confident in her ability to navigate the inevitable challenges that, at first, had filled her with self-doubt. There was so much she didn't know. There was so much she wanted to learn. A beautiful beetle, she discovered, destroyed a potato crop. A coyote ripped open a lamb's hind end. Many cats were born, and she learned a cat digs its own hole to die in. She removed herself from the world and became an enigma, no one really knew a thing about her in town. She became just another character in the story of a village. If she didn't say much, even less was said to her in return. Just as her old life had become immaterial to the new one, so did her attachment to its memories.

I've read a lot of your work, professor. Since you emailed, I did a little research, it was the most reading I've done in a while, maybe my whole life. Your work, your department, the work about your work. I found it fascinating, as I've said, to read the work *about* your work. I decided I would make up my own mind about you, though. I'm not the kind of person to let other people decide for me what and whom I should like and why. I have my own abilities for insight. I have my own dreams and my own take on things.

I read your wife's work too. She's really something isn't she. Her take on things.

She's definitely something, I said.

I think a lot about fires, floods, the end of the world, don't you? Seems like every day the end of the world gets closer and closer, and yet, it hasn't happened yet. Maybe it will happen today! Maybe we're done for. Maybe our demise is just outside that door, and we're just biding our time until it comes to call. I think the end of the world is the most compelling thing to think about these days. And we keep waiting around for it, like we want it to come.

You know, professor, I've been talking, and I've been noticing this whole time that you look depleted. You look lost, completely burned out.

I told her yes. Completely burned out. I feel dead, I told her. I'm so tired.

Perhaps there's another way I could be of help. I have a service that I don't usually mention when I'm selling a house. But I think I could let you in on it.

It's something private, something very intimate. It's not what you think it is, but it's not unthinkable either.

It's outside of what's normal, I mean.

I couldn't help but find this proposition sexy.

I have a gift, the realtor said.

But I was scared. I had learned to be frightened by my own desire.

It's a *rare* gift.

Go on, I urged her, go on.

I can speak about and validate subtleties of consciousness that are usually dismissed by the Western mind. It's something I was not taught to do, but rather it came to me. And over the past several years I have been cultivating it and helping people come to terms with *love*.

It's beyond therapy, if that's what you're thinking. Therapy is just the ego attempting to make sense of the stories it weaves and then loops on repeat. What I'm talking about is *removing* ourselves from all that. Removing ourselves from the ego. *Love*. It's a never-ending flow of wisdom.

I can see you flinching at that word, and it's because your ego has made you believe you aren't worthy of love. It's why you're here, and it's the reason I bring it up. You came here because you wanted to find love, you wanted to come back into balance with yourself. Yes, you came because you are interested in this house, but deep down, it's love you are looking for.

You think you've lost everything, but you haven't lost anything at all because you had nothing to *begin* with. None of us has anything, in fact. None of us has anything at all, and that is beautiful. This is about removing the power of the ego from the soul, removing the myth of something into the truth of everything. It isn't about *me*. Or *you*.

I asked her who it was about.

Helen.

But what did Helen have to do with it?

I can tap into a world that Helen can see and feel and experience. A world that she is connected to at the most elemental level, that I am only worthy of remarking on when I bring her fully into my consciousness. I go into a deep trance to bring her out, and then I am the body with which she teaches, and the hand with which she touches. It's Helen that brings the truth out, and I am a body able to embrace her, to channel her wisdom through my own.

But I thought Helen was the owner of this house.

It's how I introduced her to you, as the owner of this house, but this house has had so many owners...

Okay, but if Helen isn't the owner, then who is the owner? I asked.

Helen is the owner. But she's *more* than the owner, is what I'm saying.

So, who's Helen? You? And Helen is the owner?

Helen comes *through* me.

So, Helen is the owner, and she's an entity, that you channel?

That's right!

And who are you?

I'm the realtor. Helen, on the other hand, is an entity beyond ownership. If it helps you to think of her as the owner, then by all means, think of her as the owner. But ownership is a story, as everything is. To me, Helen is an entity that is pure *consciousnesses*, beyond form. She is infectious and inspires confidence and action. She is a healer, a kind of all-encompassing love.

I didn't know what to think. But I had nothing to lose from playing this game. Helen was the owner, Helen had left the city, Helen was all-encompassing love, what did I care?

It was night.

Maybe Helen was a player in this game, maybe she would appear, and we would all make love, and it would be this elemental awakening that I needed.

I was aroused, I tell you, but all over my body. It was an arousal that was beyond my body.

Okay, I said. Tell me more.

Stay here.

I need to connect with Helen, alone.

I'll come back in twenty minutes. Wait for the knock at the door. Then, you'll let me in, and I'll ask you what your name is and to repeat it three times.

That is the point at which the channeling will begin.

In the meantime, please prepare questions for her.

It's best if they come from the heart.

Don't overthink them.

ACT 3

HELEN

I opened the front door. There was the realtor, wearing a raincoat, twenty minutes later. The weather had changed. In her arms were four pieces of stovewood and an old newspaper.

She hung her coat on a mudroom hook. She came in and made a fire in the woodstove. Soon, the room warmed up, and orange glowed behind the stove glass.

The realtor asked me to sit on the built-in couch and make myself comfortable. There was something different about her, but I could not place what.

She was holding a bag, and inside it was a glass and a bottle of brown liquid. She put the glass on the table and poured the liquid into it, motioning for me to take it. She took another glass out of the same bag, poured some for herself, and drank it down quickly. I did the same.

Please speak your name three times.

I did what she said.

Okay, I'm ready for your first question.

I asked her what this was all about.

It's about your spirit, of course.

But what does that even mean?

If you look at your spirit as a horse running through a field, you can see that there's just no restrictions, there's just absolute expression without any kind of hesitation. There's just *complete expression*. The soul, on the other hand—like when a man is soulful, when he's playing jazz and he *becomes* the music—is how the essence of who we are can come through.

As the realtor talked, she closed her eyes, and every so often I could see them flutter open, exposing the whites. Her eyes were turned back inside her head. And yet, there was still something seductive about her, still, the way she sat, with her legs wide open, her hands on her knees.

Go ahead, ask another.

Is my career over?

This voice that's in your head, it's not you, professor. This voice is your ego. Your ego is trying to make you small. But, baby, you know how to write, you know what to do. All you're thinking about is your failures and your sadness. You need to *love*. You're all about work. But it's love that you need. The engine will roll, and you'll be totally fine. You need to sit in nature and let it wash over you. You need to live again. You're confined, baby, and you need to be free. You need to swim, baby. You need to jump into cold water.

Should I buy this house? Is this a test?

I need you to be serious. You've become entranced by a woman, and you're contemplating objectifying her. Is that a joke to you? The thing is, that's not *you*, that's your ego. You don't really want to penetrate her body, you want to penetrate her *consciousness*, because you have a lack of consciousness. You are empty, and you are seeking fulfillment. You think it's as simple as buying and selling but it's not, baby, it's much more complex than that. Take your wife, for example.

Your wife is what you'd call an "amiable" person. This means that underneath her easy sensibility there is a tendency to build resentment, which grows slowly over time and doesn't manifest as a problem until it's too late. Most of the time she goes about her work saying little, becoming even quieter when interrupted, losing track of what she believes, serving the whims of her superiors while quietly managing the systems of the college from a middle management position, getting none of the credit.

Do you understand?

Yes, but what does that have to do with my career?

Because like a true amiable, your wife does the work and never complains about it, and because she does it affably, no one even notices that she's the one doing it, just that it gets done. Whereas you are *noticed*. And even though her colleagues have become accustomed to the rate at which the department chugs along, they assume it's due to the upper management and their own ability to see the world from an objective and high place, able to pick out any detail. Your wife's colleagues tease her. They ask her with skepticism what she does all day. What they don't know is that because she does her work so easily, whereas it comes to them as such a struggle, it doesn't look like she struggles. And because she also doesn't complain, which they do, and often, they assume she's happy.

Look. Because many of your wife's colleagues are expressives, any time there is an opening for your wife to prove her value, they interrupt her and then forget to return to her thoughtful contribution. Eventually people who offer less to the university are promoted above her, and she grows resentful. But because your wife's supervisors have gotten so used to her even demeanor, they bristle all the more at what appears to them as her growing self-righteousness. She applies to fellowships so that she might transcend her work through her craft, but she receives many rejections.

The only thing left for her to do is to take her frustration out on you.

Isn't that right, baby?

I said that yes, my wife took out her frustrations on me.

Right, because she's been overlooked. She's been *badly* overlooked. And eventually when you proved to be an even more indifferent audience than the world itself, your wife turned to what I can only assume is a classic amiable breakdown. In other words, she left you. But, before this even happened, you had started to drift away yourself, somewhere in body and soul. You forgot you had any desire at all, anywhere, especially in your marriage but also in other parts of life. You retreated, daydreaming, staring into space, looking at your feet, rearranging the stacks of paper on your desk and engaging passively in faculty meetings. And even though most of the work done by your students was uninspired, you took more time reviewing it, and even though you were procrastinating more than working, thinking about working took up enough time so that you never felt like you had enough time to do it.

You are always without time, with too much work, regardless of how much time or how little work you actually have. It's because you struggle with purpose, baby. You do things because you *have to*, but that's the only reason. If you didn't need to do things, you wouldn't bother doing anything at all. What kind of life is that? A life without meaning?

I told her that, in fact, I had wondered if there was even a point to existing. I had thought that observing, and then creating work based on those observations—making—was my way into the truth of existing. But was it just as possible ceasing to exist was the only way to exist truthfully?

That's why, in terms of energy, leaving the city would be a positive move for you. You need support, you need nature, you're needing more of a natural kind of energy, and you're not getting it. It's the internal energy that is within each of us. Part of you, part of your teaching has been to put as much money aside as you can so that you can arrive at a moment and say, "Now I'm ready, I'm going to do it." But who is "I"?

I thought I would remain relevant forever. But will I?

You need to see what happens next. You were working at a terrible place. I'm not sure that education is a safe business for you to be in. You need to figure out what makes sense for you and what you can do and what you can't do. If there are fifteen things that need to be done, you do all fifteen things. You have no balance. You're an addict. Always hustling. You're a beautiful addict, and a very loving addict, but you're still an addict. You do too much. I think it's beautiful, baby, but it doesn't have a long-term lifespan, because you're going to burn yourself out. You need to do less and do it more fully.

You need to think of life as a pond, and caretake the edges of the pond, diving in whenever you get hot. But a "pond" is something you have to teach *yourself*, baby. It's not something I can tell you. What I can tell you is that it's because of *compassionate reasons* you're looking for it.

My wife. Why am I not attracted to her?

What you're asking me is bullshit. Baby, why don't you *know* her? You're a very loving, compassionate person. You've got something real there. You understand? You're a very loving, very compassionate person. And your wife is in control. And so, you're frustrated with her, and it looks like she's repulsive because she has what you yearn for, and you have to reject it out of *pain*. She's messier than you, she has emotions and feelings, she is run by desire, and you don't have that range.

What you're really saying to me is "I wish I could just express part of my emotions and just be *like* my wife." You want to be like her, and you want her. You're telling me you don't, but you do. You want your wife, badly! What do you think your wife would say to you?

She'd say I was being naïve.

See, there's that voice in your head giving you this information.

You don't know a part of yourself, and at this age you should know the qualities of your heart. And you don't. You doubt your own heart! And you compare it. Part of your ego is throwing you off because you're comparing apples and oranges. Your wife is with you because of the quality of your heart. She married you because of the qualities of *you*. It's *yourself* who repulses you, baby.

But my wife is so angry. Why does she resent me?

Because she should. But baby, it's still false information. Your ego is giving you false information. When this happens to you, you need to say to yourself: *This is not correct*. Your wife—and I really, truly believe your wife loves you. I genuinely believe she just absolutely loves you. What she has difficulty with is when you have *uncertainties* inside you. I know, it has not been easy.

But I believe on an intimate level, on a sensual level, on a sexual level—you need to get on track. You guys need to bond more.

Sexually?

On every level.

How?

You take your clothes off, and you take her pants off, and you just do it. You have to *enter her*.

In the past, she's been the wind and you've been the feather. Roles change, characters change, it's part of the evolution of a marriage. I think she's very grounded. I think she's doing things to create grounding, to stabilize everything. But she has to be the guide now. You have to follow her. She's been following you. Now it's her turn to lead.

You're saying I should work on things with my wife?

You guys need to have much more *sex*, is what I'm saying. When was the last time you put her on a massage table and just pleasured her? I don't care if you watch porn, I don't care if you get more toys. I don't care—the woman is pretty open! It's not that she's not willing... she's pretty open sexually. She's alive, she's fully *there*.

What if I'm afraid of her?

You're afraid of a deeper level of intimacy with her. You're afraid of being vulnerable, baby. She's stronger than you. You have to let her be the strong one.

Why do I find myself fantasizing about her as her younger self?

Because it's something you can control. When you imagine her this way, it's because you can *control* the experience. You don't feel safe with her now because she's stronger than you. And when we don't feel safe, that's what we do. You need to have a very honest conversation and say to your wife: "What's going to please you? Tell me what you like." You might say, "I want anal sex, do you?" or you might say "I want you to get a strap on, and I want you to penetrate me." You might ask to be caressed. You might caress *her* with a flower. But you have to figure out what you *want*, and you have to be curious about what *she* wants.

You're changing and evolving, and none of this is shameful.

But you're cold, baby. You're so cold!

But what if I want to be with another woman?

I will tell you, even if you told your wife you wanted to experiment with other people, I think you would have a really good experience, and maybe even she would have a good experience, and you would be very turned on, and within no time you would say, "No, I don't want this." You would be back where you started. Listen, go back to your wife, baby.

Go back.

Look.

All your life you have been like a child in a classroom drawing pictures on a worksheet. "If I could only be a better student," you say, "I could make my teacher happy." But you are the teacher, too, and you are also like a child, wandering in a meadow. The teacher in you thinks, "how did I wind up a teacher when I am also a child?" You might say, if you have enough of something to be content not to worry about the basic logistics of living, the mind inevitably goes to a place of desire.

"What is the thing I don't have," you are saying to yourself, "and how can I get it?" The mind is fickle, and the mind fixates, soon it is the desired thing in relation to the stable thing. Life becomes a choice: which do I want more? What would make me happier? And if I choose one and it's the wrong choice, what then? I'd have had it all and thrown it all away.

But what's the use in choosing between two things that might not lead to happiness? You can't be fickle about it, that's all I can say. You don't choose between survival and death when it comes to finding happiness. And you can't be fickle about *living*.

That's it.

That's the end.

She looked at her watch, stretched her arms behind her back, then turned out the light.

The room went black.

ACT 4

HELEN AND MAN

My mother had a set of china which I always thought would explode if I touched it, or that, if I used it incorrectly, would detonate a world war. Maybe she used it on special occasions with guests long after I was asleep. But I never saw it move beyond its encasement in the sacred hutch.

When my mother died, my wife and I inherited the china. What a burden to be the benefactor of these potential catastrophes. A responsibility had been bequeathed to me: Don't mess this up, I didn't, now it's up to you. And what should happen if I broke it, one piece, or all of it in some inevitable earthquake? A chasm would open beneath me and suck me down forever. And if I sold it, the china would become an object of undervalued importance, something worthy of anyone. How much could I realistically get for it and what would I use it for, the returns? Something with no history, with nothing attached to it, something whose journey did not have pain etched into it, whose wellbeing had not been attended to in other countries, had not been packed lovingly, had not been an artifact of family, had not made it across an ocean, had not survived for decades in cabinets. Something without honor, something made without pain, or made with a pain that had less to do with survival.

After a few hours, as if struck by lightning, I was awake and surrounded by unfamiliar darkness. The whiskey, or whatever it was, had knocked me into a stupor. I was lying down and my arm was hanging off the edge of the built-in couch.

I was alone. I was still in the house.

I got up, made my way to the mudroom in the dark, found my coat on the hook, and checked my phone. It was 2 a.m. The realtor was right, there was no internet.

I could see without turning on the light, not that I would have even known where a light switch would be. And yet, perhaps if I had known, I would have left it off anyway.

I was still furry, but my adrenaline was coursing. I knew where I had been—on the built-in—but I had forgotten why. I debated driving back to my hotel, but it was cold, the air had gotten brisk, there was a wind inside, I could see there was snow falling and it had become serious. I went closer to the fire, which was almost entirely out. I looked at the door to the deck and saw it had blown open. I got up, went over to the door, and shut it, a bit of snow coming with it. This act of walking and shutting and doing took courage.

When I returned, there was a woman on the built-in.

As I opened my mouth to say something, she held up her hand. Something in me clarified, as if the woman were speaking to me, but without words.

I was frightened. Who was this person and who was I, where was this person and where was I, was I in danger?

There was no way for me to have known who she was. And yet I did, the way one knows everything, or nothing, in a dream. The way nothing makes sense and yet it all fits together, the ordered chaos of detail, the disordered chaos of time passing, of time failing to pass.

I knew it was Helen because it was Helen, and that was all I needed to know.

I said her name aloud. I heard myself say it. She looked at me as if to say yes.

She didn't look exactly like the realtor, and yet there was a strange resemblance. She was older, there was a wisdom to her, and the way she held her body was different. Their clothes were different. But their faces were almost similar. Almost similar and yet also different.

She leaned back on the built-in and put her feet straight out, ankles crossed, hands behind her head, elbows out. She looked right at me, like a man looking at another man.

Helen was at assisted living, or Helen had died—I couldn't remember if she was dead or in assisted living—and yet here she was, neither frigid nor translucent. She was Helen, sitting on the built-in, as if I had been waiting for her. As if she had been there all the while as I slept, and only now had I become aware of her.

I sat on the floor, cross legged, with my hands on my knees. I leaned over, as if to summon all the breath I had. I looked up at her. She looked down at me.

Suddenly I was overcome with the memory of the day my wife had left me. It was an intrusive thought. An intimate thought. It was a memory of the moment where I had lost everything.

It was this memory that dominated my mind, instead of the fear of whatever Helen, whatever she was that was possibly here to injure me, or possibly here to rob me, someone who had been watching me sleep, who had broken into the house, or who had been there all along.

But from the place in which my memory resided, a place of purity emerged somehow, and I spoke to her without fear.

My voice was hot and fast.

I've been thinking about the day my wife left me. The worst day of my life.

I had just come back from my morning walk.

It was terribly cold in our house, and because of the wind from my walk I remember I had streaks of tears on my face. I came in from my walk, cold and colder, and my wife was sitting at the table, dressed and upright, formal. She told me she was leaving me.

She told me she had realized there was a vast difference between us, the way we thought, a difference that had become too deep and disturbing. She said for years it had been as though she were walking on a thin log over a rushing creek hundreds of feet below, only to realize that there had been a sign all along that said, "DANGEROUS:

GOATS ONLY." She realized she wasn't a goat.

She realized she valued her life on the day-to-day. A good day meant all was okay, while a bad day was cause for concern. She said she held onto the good days knowing they had been out-weighed by the bad days for years. She realized that I thought about the long view, about life over a long period of time, not by moments, but by the concept of it in general; a completed vision of what I hoped it would be in the end.

She said that she was leaving me then, but in fact had decided to leave me many years ago.

She described a meal we had, years back, on the deck of a house we had rented for the summer. She had just rescued her dog—it was her dog, although we lived together. It had come from a beach, a street dog with jutting ribs who was now well-fed. The dog was a scrounger and would jump onto tables the minute your back was turned and devour everything in sight. I had never come around to it. I would sit in my upstairs office all summer and hear the squeaking of the wooden table as the dog walked all over it, licking the surface for crumbs. In truth, I disliked the dog. You could say I strongly disliked it.

The meal was in honor of our friends who had come up for the weekend from the city. The dog was behaving badly as usual—no amount of gentle scolding would register, and our friends seemed to encourage her, commenting on how adorable she was, her human-like eyes, the way she seemed to see into their souls. She was a small dog, smooth and long-bodied, a fox's tail, bright gold ears that she held back as if in a low ponytail, and a sweet, honest face. When she slept, she curled into a ball like a cat. These were details, they said, that should have endeared me to her. But they did not.

During dessert that evening, the dog jumped onto the table for the hundredth time and, without thinking, I struck her forcefully, knocking the dog off the table. She ricocheted off the wooden bench.

That was the moment my wife decided to leave me. And yet it was years until she actually did.

She told me, also, that she realized we approached our emotional and intellectual lives in opposing ways, and it went beyond just our perspective of relationships. She discovered, after years of resentment and fog, that she was like an anchor. Her tendency was to sink down low into the depths, as she was an introvert and valued her time alone. She was rooted in what felt real, like the floor of an ocean or lake. She was the kind of person who kept ships from drifting away.

But I was like a kite, my wife told me. I was only happy when I was flying, abstract and loose, my bold colors and plumage free and liberated, blowing with the wind, me looking out over the world from high above it.

She said that despite being opposites, anchors and kites made sense together, for the obvious reason that a kite cannot fly forever, or it will fly away, and an anchor would sink too deep and get locked in the muck. We needed each other to exist fully. This had been a comfort to her over the years, despite her bad feelings.

But over the course of time, my wife told me she had begun to feel her anchor-ness in a new way, and that my kite-ness tugged her up at times she didn't want to be tugged up. She said that I had been flying more and more, needing to be held in place by her for longer and longer periods, so that she was anchoring for stretches of time that did not feel fair to her, even though when given a reprieve she was fully content to stay put, just as long as it was on her terms. She realized that while an anchor's main purpose was to hold a ship in place, it wasn't meant to *solely* anchor—it had every right, and in fact *demanded* to be pulled up from time to time to rest on deck and enjoy the feeling of the open air. This didn't mean the kite had to stop flying, but at times it would have been nice for her to lay coiled on the deck without having to work so hard.

It was the case that for too long, I—the kite—had become tangled in a high tree, and she—the anchor—had been pulled at constantly with no predictable pattern. She saw the reality that I would likely never become disentangled as I was very badly knotted.

She was done being an anchor entirely.

She was ready to be a kite, too, in fact.

There was no point arguing my reasons for how she could be a kite and how I—once I had become disentangled—could become an anchor for her, how we could swap positions. She did not want to be anchored by me, she told me, as I was not capable. A kite can never become an anchor, only anchors could become kites.

I heard Helen laugh.

It was unclear to me how much of what I had said was internal, as so many details appeared in front of me like I was watching them in a film. I could explain them with such detail, and yet it was possible I had just seen them in my own mind.

I saw now she had a small dog on her lap, white with a brown spot over its eye, lithe, with tiny feet, the size of a giant rat. She stroked the dog's head.

I continued.

But isn't that stupid? Anything can become anything else. Everything already *is* everything else. Only the mind makes distinctions between kites or anchors, and the mind is itself unreal.

These were my words, I had spoken them, but they didn't necessarily feel like my thoughts.

Suddenly, Helen's dog hopped off the couch and proceeded to race around the room on what I now saw was only three legs.

It ran without difficulty, grunting with pleasure, breathing hard, leaning almost parallel to the ground, around the circumference of the large room again and again, smiling in a joyous grimace, racing around in circles, each circle getting progressively smaller, until by the end, it was chasing its tail in a tight turn, nearly dancing on point at Helen's feet. When it finished, it hopped up and sat on the built-in, panting. Helen stroked the dog's ears lovingly, from forehead to ear tip.

My career is over!

I made a point to say this loudly, as I didn't know if I were speaking or thinking, and yet it was clear she could hear me, regardless of whether the words were, in fact, coming out of my mouth.

Helen looked at me, nodding.

It is clear to me now that "nature" and "trees" is more about writing to communicate things to myself that otherwise would have come to harm me if left to fester. That I have been writing to free myself from the preoccupations that trapped me in a kind of intellectual misery, and I have been using these beautiful, natural beings as props. It's sad, really, the way I have implemented such gorgeous flowers.

Back when people responded favorably to my work, I became sated, the way someone here might be congratulated at the dump for a truckload of cast-off metal dug out of the woods. I would have spurts of imaginative impulse; I'd stay up late and wake up early to work, keeping up time with what felt like endless revelations, each brought on by an uncomfortable event—a rejection, a feared rejection, a fight with my wife, some amalgamation of doubt that had been eating at me and for whatever reason had reached the tenderest point. I'd be comforted by relaying it to paper, creating a kind of elegant testimonial that responded to some traumatic event as if confiding in an objective, secret listener who passed no judgment. I'd read it over days later when the feeling had passed, and not recall any amount of the wrenching I had embodied so heartily. The words existed as if totally apart from me, so I was able to excise myself from the pain they made. I was captaining the ship, I had my own anchor, I was capable of healthy distances from storms, and from the tendencies to pick and pick at scabs. Certainly, none of the writers on whom I modelled myself were such anxious wrecks as I was, and I was ashamed of my insecurities.

There were weeks when my wife and I fought constantly about nothing, hating each other's predictability—endless feelings of ire and rancor, if she would just shut the fuck up!—and these were times when I wrote more, and passionately, as if in spite of her boredom of me, and her inability to honor the values which I found crucial, her distaste for all my periodicals on the small kitchen table, a piece of furniture whose purpose was indecipherable except as a surface to gather magazines, and yet for some reason which she felt must always be cleared of stuff. My wife would relocate my magazines to a place out of easy reach and then chastise me for being annoyed about their relocation.

She was always menstruating or about to menstruate or recovering from menstruating, and I reminded her of it when her time was coming, for I had tuned in so devotedly to her cycle I could predict an outburst. I wanted her to feel seen, to prove I could see her that clearly. It had become a kind of astrology. I could make decisions based on the implications of her date and time as if in angle to the sun. And this angered her. Me, seeing her clearly!

Then there were the times when we were happy. Those were the worst times for writing. I never wrote when happy. These were times I played, times I didn't bother to record, the long hours by the water and the beers I drank. How I loved her then for her predictability, and yet I never wrote about it because I wasn't grappling and I couldn't stew in it, for it was sparkling and lucid. When I tried to write during these times, I would disgust myself and think, this is the end of my inspiration, I'll never write again, I guess it was happiness I was after and now I've found it, I can be done with writing forever. But then something would erupt, and we'd have an argument, and rage and fear would return and there my words would be as if waiting to prove that it was them all along—the suffering of feeling, of being agonizing and of agony itself—that gave my life meaning, as opposed to the joy, which was a balm against truth.

I could appreciate the idea that joy and pain lived side by side and that happiness was not one without the presence of the other, that they informed each other. But what did it say about me that I found purpose in unhappiness, that I was always wanting more of it, and that the more I had the more I desired, the more I thought I needed?

My wife would go into the guest room and shut the door and I'd hear her watching the shows she knew I hated, and I'd question myself, what did I need, exactly? Why did we find each of our ideas so uninteresting? Why did I watch gory films when I was angry? Films that were all about dominating women when she was watching slow and lovely movies about women in houses, women married to other women, women on the run from men, female anthropologists falling in love with robots.

I was well-versed in selfishness. I was well-versed in the practice, especially as it related to ambition. But I lived with a palpable sense of emptiness. Like right before an explosion. Like the creaking of weight-bearing walls just before the building comes down. There was doom, a feeling of impending disaster. My wife said it had to do with energy, a kind of energy rut.

I fucked her every now and then, and always with my eyes closed, imagining her as a younger woman. I kept my eyes closed. I thought to myself, everyone keeps their eyes closed. Pancake ass, she was the woman who ruined me, then I'd think of her young, supple body and the way she used to walk, and I could think about it for hours and be happy, like a child reading comics on the beach.

You have to be careful these days. So unbelievably careful. Everyone's on everyone else's case. Everything can become litigious at the drop of a hat. It got to the point where you couldn't trust your own ideas anymore! My wife didn't trust my ideas anymore. She had been taken in by the women who were afraid of my nuanced simplicity. It was actually a complex philosophy, but these women oversimplified everything. They were simpleminded, and my wife had taken to them. They had ruined my life by taking her in. She had ruined my life by being taken in by them.

My ideas now seemed to be for an audience I would never win over. I had the degrees and the awards, but it was like my sentences were fragmented and therefore cast aside like they were incomplete, or if they were read carefully, they were criticized brutally. I began writing with very wide margins and loose spacing as if to take up space and move through the pages of my notebook faster, toward something of an end goal, some result I could take pride in, something complete, a sense of having achieved finality. Or maybe it was the feeling of looseness, of letting my words take up space.

And why shouldn't they, what had soured the world on my words?

Was it acceptable to continue a practice of writing about nature when my version of nature had come under attack? No one seemed to want my side of the story. They made it seem like it was my story they were trying to move away from. It seemed that I was a victim of a fickle economy, an industry that only cared about exceptionalism. That suddenly the mosses themselves were looked down upon, but they were everything but small, and that the mundaneness of nature somehow didn't matter and I was no longer seen as shiny, and I wanted to be shiny again. I'll admit it, I didn't understand the feeling of dullness. They wanted new ideas, they said, well, I was having new ideas, wasn't I? No, they didn't think so.

My wife would ask me for a back rub, and I would look at my pen. She would say, "You're hardly getting any words down on the page," and, "You're wasting paper, your handwriting has gotten so big." It was my right, I told her, to take up space! Now I know that too many times I would say, "Hold on," and then would write to finish my thought, and she'd have fallen asleep before I could do any back rubbing.

Failure. That's where I was. It's where I had been. I had to admit this to myself, that I had become unsuccessful, that I was chasing after something unattainable that I had once attained but since misplaced. I had a feeling of having been somewhere, not knowing how to get back, like understanding the route but not the means of transport. Rooted in failure like a root in cement, cemented in failure like a pillar in an ugly house, pillared in my inadequacy which was endless and vast. My wife saw it and she had fled, from me, and from my failure.

I was rotten, ruined.

I had always been the kind of man who considered himself kind. I lived my life this way, saying yes to people, as I enjoyed and felt comfort and safety in their relief to be given the thing they needed. It was that way with my wife who wasn't pleased to come in second to my ambitions, and so I showered her with agreements: "Yes" to all the things she wanted, to all the linens and the dishes and the art. "Yes," to every garment, to streaming services for old films, the carpet cleaning, and the vacations to places I had no interest in visiting. I knew I needed to say "Yes" because she deserved to be happy, and my "Yes" seemed to me my only means of making her so.

She would thank me, she would say the word "love," but my yesses did not really make her happy. She told me it was as if I had orchestrated the state of sadness and abandonment for the sake of my career, and that my generosity was a lie, used to distract her from the injustice I was systemizing so I could sweep in with "Yes" and solve her problems and bring her peace so that she would stop bothering me with her desire. But no, I told her, I gave because I was generous and because I loved her, not because I wanted to appear to be loving, not because I wanted to trap her in a web of misery, but because I cared for her.

"You love only yourself," my wife said, "you love others as a way to love *yourself*, to prove you can love at all. But caring is not something you do," she said, "care is something you give." And while I had been technically caring for years, I had never really *given* her care at all, and that was why she was leaving.

But I cared! I cared deeply.

My wife said, no, it was all a lie, the yesses were really nos and I was a "No" person, and she was looking for happiness.

Helen jumped up. It was clear she was on my side.

Betrayal!

As she got up to her feet, the dog flew off her lap.

She was shouting. They were her words now, but they felt like mine, too, somehow.

Betrayal!

As if she didn't know exactly who she married! As if you had changed, when in fact it was *she* who had changed, but the blame fell on *you*!

The dog began to race around the room again, this time grunting with its face in a tight grimace, its tail up, its missing leg rooting its body through some phantasmic force, around and around the room three times almost parallel to the floor. When it finished, again it hopped up, breathing heavily, and again seated itself next to Helen, who had sat back down.

She petted its neck and ear, like before, and continued.

It's just these people who think they know the way the world should work. They're all the same people, the same kind.

Her voice was thicker than the realtor's, rhythmic and soothing.

When you live here, you'll have community, and you'll think they're different than your colleagues, but they're not different, they're all the same.

There's a pond, you know, right down the hill. When you live here you'll have to ask yourself, will you share it with the neighbors?

For example, I told one of my neighbors that her son should use my pond on hot days. It was the right thing to do. I wanted to be generous, even though I wanted to be left alone. I wanted to be neighborly. The *right thing* was to be neighborly. The lakes had been treated, you see, for an invasive plant, during the hottest days of summer, and they were closed to the public. I told my neighbor that her son was welcome to come to my pond and swim, but that he should be careful, that he should make sure to shut the door on the little cabin should he come in the afternoon, so the mice didn't take over and eat the towels.

Helen was caressing her dog. Her legs were crossed. She removed her sweater, and I saw that it had mended elbows. She set it down on the built-in beside her.

I was still sitting cross-legged on the floor, looking up at her.

She picked up my drink, finished it, and leaned back.

I said to my neighbor, if your son forgets to close the cabin door, it's not the end of the world, the mice will find a way in through a crack or a window regardless.

It was very hot. For over a week, the boy didn't come. I figured he didn't want to impose, maybe she hadn't even told him, maybe she didn't want him having that kind of independence, swimming with his friends far out of earshot. I'll be honest with you, I was relieved. I thought, well, I'd offered it. And it was they who had decided not to take me up on my offer. They couldn't accuse me of being ungenerous, a flatlander with a nice pond who posts her land, who hoards her potatoes in the famine. At least I had offered, and yet I was happy no one had come because I didn't really want to share, I had only wanted to extend the invitation and have them ignore it.

Maybe the boy told his mother about the time he saw me swimming naked, that other time he'd come by to swim without an invitation. I hadn't rushed to cover myself up, I was at the end of the dock with no access to a towel, and when he saw me, he ran away. Maybe the mother felt I had some kind of interest in the boy, some desire to expose myself to him, that I was a predator. But then I thought, she couldn't possibly think I wanted anything to do with her son, I was practically a grandmother! Of course, the mother must have known I hadn't meant that the boy should come swimming *with* me, just that should he feel the need to cool off, and that because the lakes had been closed, that he and maybe some of his friends should feel free to jump into the pond without feeling the need to call me and *ask*. It was an open invitation to share resources! Eventually, I stopped worrying about it. I enjoyed my swimming pond and was glad to be alone, with the feeling that my solitude had been morally earned.

But two weeks later, almost when I had forgotten about the invitation entirely, the boy came. One afternoon, with some friends. I could hear them all the way from the house, as the sound traveled up the hill. They were hooting and hollering and having a grand old time, and in a way, it was pleasant to hear young people enjoying themselves in the water.

But I was also troubled. It affected what I felt I was able to do myself; I found it hard to imagine going down to swim at the same time as they were swimming, and then immediately I found myself waiting for them to leave, I would be picking at threads in the cushions inside, waiting for sounds of the jumping and yelling to stop. When there was a break in sound, I would be relieved, maybe they had gone. But they must have been playing a hiding game because the yelling would suddenly resume.

The first day, the boys left around dinnertime. And when I went down to swim, the water was still moving and it felt tarnished somehow, the tension on the water's surface had been broken and it was oily, or soapy, or because the surface had been rippled, the water felt different when my body struck the surface, I didn't get the normal shock of cold. And although it could have been because of how humid the day was, I attributed it to the boys and their bodies heating up the water.

They came back the next day. And the next. Both hot days where people would normally spend an entire day at the lake, but of course, the lakes were closed. All day they played with a volleyball, jumped off the dock, paddled around in floating rafts they must have brought along. They were using the pond just as I had offered it, just as I had suggested they use it. This went on for some weeks, over the hottest days of summer.

The lakes had to have been ready. Why hadn't they gone back to the lakes, and met up with their friends? But of course, the boys liked my pond because they could walk there and because they could be there without parents. I had never come down while they were swimming so they likely felt entirely separate and confident and satisfied in their own private paradise, why would they go back to the lakes when they were reliant on their parents for rides there and back, so they had to wait around for what would work with their parents' schedules? With my pond they only had to make up their own minds because it was close enough to ride their bikes. They didn't think about *me* wanting to use the pond. They didn't stop to think, is this the moment that Helen will want to swim, in this heat? They had no idea I wanted to use the pond, but of course I wanted to use it, it was hot out and it was a beautifully cold pond.

The truth was, I did use the pond.

I got my time in early, before any of them got up and ate breakfast, and then later in the evenings when the surface tension righted itself, after they left.

Anyway, the boys came every day one week when I was making hay, and I didn't have time to think about them. I only noticed they had been there because of the orientation of the chairs, the arrangement of the sand, and the other smaller things that had shifted during their visit. But they never left any trash, they always closed the cabin door, and in general were respectful and courteous.

I had to admit, the pond was a pretty good example of the commons.

But one day, I got a phone call. My neighbor told me a boy had been taken to the hospital, did I know they had been drinking at the pond? I had no idea. Yes, they had been drinking and playing in the water and one of the boys had pushed another one's head under and he was drunk enough that he passed out and they had to give him CPR and one of them ran home and she had driven them all to the hospital. "Thank goodness I was home," my neighbor said, "He could have died."

I told her I was happy to hear that everything had turned out okay with the boy, and that she must have been terrified. "You should have known they were drinking," my neighbor said. "You should have paid closer attention."

It was outrageous! This had nothing to do with me! They had let their children purchase or steal alcohol. They had let their children run free. They had allowed them to risk their lives and it was not my job to take care of them, that was not the deal we had made. I explained this to the mother, and said my house was way too far from the pond to even know the details other than hearing distant shouting, and I had been haying that week so was on my tractor and therefore could hear nothing except the sound of my own thoughts, and just barely. Did they really expect me to go down there and check up on the boys? Ridiculous, I said to the woman.

Then she told me they were planning to press charges because it was my pond, because one of the boys had almost died within earshot of my house and because of my *negligence*, letting the children play in the pond and drink alcohol in the pond. As if it was my duty to watch over them, and I should have to pay. I said I couldn't be held responsible for them swimming and I had assumed their parents were okay with it. I had invited the boy through *you*, I said to her, his *mother*.

I was furious and for a second, I thought about moving, can you imagine. I called another of the mothers, but she agreed with the first one, that I had risked the boy's life, that because of my *negligence*, they used that word again, a child was nearly killed. I explained my reasoning and told the mothers they should watch out that her children weren't doing worse things, where did they get the alcohol anyway, had they checked their own cabinets to see what else was missing? If they hadn't been drinking, I said, everything would have been fine, it wasn't up to me to make sure they abided by the law, and they should be careful I didn't report the mothers to the state, they should be careful that I didn't send over a truancy officer to do a welfare check! I said it probably was obvious that the boys were not invited to return to the pond.

And indeed, the boys never came again.

I should never have invited them.

There's a price one pays for being generous.

So, just be careful.

You know, this house has been in my family for eighty years. Eighty years, and I wanted to *move*, because of these boys. My aunt bought this house when she came over just after the war, when it was a rundown old farm. Back then the pond wasn't even there. I dug the pond myself, years later.

My aunt was generous. She would have let the boys use the pond, no question. But she would have watched them closely. She would have seen it coming, not like me, my head in the tractor spokes, my head all greased up with the importance of the land when the land doesn't need anyone to worry about it.

My aunt had seen a lot of terrible things. Things that make our stories seem like jokes. She never spoke of these things, but later I learned.

Like when a group of soldiers threw small children by their hair and limbs into the back of a truck, like stray dogs.

Helen got up suddenly and grabbed me by the hair, yanking my head back. Her dog growled, and she spat on me.

Like this! Only imagine you were a *toddler*.

I allowed Helen to hold my hair for a long time, until my neck was in such pain that I cried out. It was what I had wanted, that kind of pain. The kind of real, earned emotion. It was horrible, and yet it was earned.

She released me.

My aunt was involved in an effort to save people. She worked with an underground network, picking babies up at train stations and delivering them to safety. She herself was not in need of saving, but she put herself at great risk to save others.

A man who needed saving and his two young children who needed saving moved in with her. A writer, in fact. Like you.

During the day my aunt posed as wife and mother and they all lived in the main quarters of the house, but during the night the father and his children slept in the servants' quarters. Every day they practiced hiding, perfecting a routine should there be a raid, which consisted of a pit my aunt had dug underneath the floorboards below the coffee table. To keep the writer's children quiet in the pit, she would dose them with sleeping powder. She would say, my husband and my children, they aren't here, they are visiting my mother. They practiced this like a sport. They made a game of it. It marked the passage of time.

One evening, my aunt and the writer were involved in a game of chess while the children played by the fire. They were captivated by strategy and, because of the snow, did not hear the car pull up to the house. She barely had enough time to move the family safe into the pit, and yet, somehow, she managed to get them hidden in time.

It was an officer who came to the door, an infamous brute, loathed by all, the worst of his kind. He searched the house, then left once he confirmed it was empty, other than my aunt. But he performed a dirty trick, returning an hour later when the writer and his children had come out and gotten comfortable again. The officer returned and busted down the door.

But my aunt was prepared. She picked up a revolver from a nearby bookshelf and shot the officer in the head. Then she hid the officer's body in the baker's wagon, and a friend helped her conceal it in someone else's coffin at the morgue. No one found out. This was likely only one of many similar stories, but my aunt did not like to discuss such things.

I always keep guns in the house, by the way, and if you live here, you should keep guns in the house, too. You never know when you'll need a gun like the day my aunt needed one.

Helen pointed her thumb and forefinger at me.

BANG!

That's right. The element of surprise!

The writer had been working on an important philosophical text. He was writing a book about human potential. The moment one thinks of anything, it becomes possible.

I was so tired. The floor was hard. Immediately, as if she was anticipating it, Helen shoved her dog off the built-in and got up, offering me her seat.

Get up.

Lie down.

I did what she said. Helen went over to the stove and added another log. She opened the flue and the fire roared. She added one more log and closed the door, then returned to the built-in. There was orange light reflecting off the stove glass.

Close your eyes.

I obeyed, like a child obeys at bedtime. Nothing felt strange, it was simply the world I was in.

Helen's dog jumped up and settled itself between my feet. The dog let out a big sigh; I could feel it relax, and I, too, became relaxed.

Then I felt a great weight on my stomach, pressing down on my bladder. I wondered if the dog was lying on top me, or if Helen was on top of me.

I opened my eyes. It was a large crystal bowl, the size of a cauldron, sitting on my stomach.

This is sound.

Pure sound, in its entirety.

It works with your body in amazing ways.

Helen struck the bowl with a mallet and a resonant hum came from within it. She ran the mallet around the outside of the bowl, pressing the soft head around and around the edge, so the sound increased its intensity and became deafening, but harmonious. The bowl vibrated with sound, and I felt the vibration in my body.

Close your eyes.

You need to stop hiding. You need to awaken.

Calling forth the woman who ruined your life. Calling forth your wife.

I was in a room of complete sound. The sound was in my body. I could not think of anything but the sound, punctuated by Helen's voice. Her words seemed to enter the crystal bowl, and their meaning vibrated down into my cells.

For all your life, your mother has been behind you. Holding you from your shirt, keeping you from moving forward and yet holding you back. But you have been unable to see her.

The woman who ruined your life has taken the place of your mother, and you must remove her. She is your wife, but she is not the woman you think she is. This is not your maternal energy. You must ask the woman who ruined your life to step away.

Calling forth the women who ruined your career. Calling forth the way they asked you to abide by the rules they then accused you of breaking.

Calling forth this betrayal. Of your essence, of the real you. The you who just wants to be loved.

Watch the women as they pack a large bag, full of clothing and books.

Watch them as they get on a bus. Watch them as they leave.

There they are. They're going now. They're all on the same bus.

Calling forth the bus the women get on. Here it is.

See the bus, the orange stripe down the side. Calling forth the bus driver, who opens the door for the women. Each woman puts her bag on the bus and sits down. They are going away, forever.

Helen rubbed the mallet against the crystal bowl, in patterns of three or four. I was bathed in the sound of the crystal, the sound of her voice. It was a feeling of ecstasy, of such incredible warmth. I felt the body of her dog between my feet. I felt a growing heat in my center, and a growing heat on my head. I felt the sun, bathing its light on me, even though it was night.

How light can you be?

Calling forth the road the bus is traveling on.

It is smooth. The pavement is freshly paved, and the bus is taking the women who ruined your life away. One of them leans her arm out the window.

Calling forth her arm, the way it waves back at you, as you bid her—as you bid all of the women—farewell.

The heat was building now, and the pressure in my center was increasing. The weight of the bowl was beginning to press down, deeper, so far deep into my body, so deep was the feeling of the dog between my feet, the sensation of the sun's light on my face. I was in ecstasy. The women were driving away on the bus. I was watching them drive away.

I was so light.

And I was overcome with thought.

I was speaking inside of myself. And yet I was sure Helen could hear me.

I thought, or I spoke.

But it didn't matter, because the words existed, and they had a witness.

Those days, when people came to me with praise or admiration, I retreated into self-doubt, preferring to believe they were only doing so to ridicule me.

I had lost my dignity and had become a clown playing out the drama of my own life. I could trust only toxicity. There was a lack of good faith—relationships felt unstable and unsure, and that I could not trust anyone, isolating myself from people who would otherwise embrace me, allow me to grow, to be simply who I was, encourage me to accept myself.

It was either a shrewd, self-aware intelligence I had achieved that kept me in sync with the darkness of life, or a kind of illogical, misanthropic paranoia, a deep fear of my own lovelessness, which held me back from happiness, despite my access to it.

It was a place of utter certainty, that even the questions had to be dissected in order that their deeper essence be known. But nothing, not even an essence, could transform into energy without an embodiment. Words could elucidate but they could not *center*. They slipped through my fingers like water returning to its source.

Words had failed me. But now I know, it *should* be difficult.

I was so calm, utterly present. And I spoke within myself, from this place of presence.

To be awake depended on the level at which I was able to sink. And I could not see the liveliness of the world because I was waiting for it to metamorphosize from larva straight to moth, forgetting that for weeks it had to crawl about as food for birds.

I had not revealed myself, my true form, had not let myself experience the world, but had hidden in a shroud of pride and timidity, a chilly empathy that masked a hunger for warmth—for love—and my students had witnessed this. They had been watching, embedding it in their codes for learning, a cunning dismay that I had modeled, a dismay that saw itself as confidence, that talked without listening. Knowledge, I had taught them, was property.

Yes, I had taught them that knowledge was a marker of status. And it had to accumulate. It offered security and possibility. I taught them the virtues of investing in a theory that remained consistent with the self I encouraged them to curate. I called it "true nature," but it was false, in fact, and I had celebrated them for perfecting it.

To do the work of being awake, one has to live in a dual space, to reside also in the shadow of a house so that daytime appeared dark and gray, despite our knowing that on the other side of the house was plentiful sunshine.

And my wife? For years she had let me choose the make and model of every car we bought out of a kind of engendered deference. She had made marks on the discipline, through her research, and yet she had not been appreciated in her profession. She had not achieved advancement. She had no curricular control over the department in which we both resided, and her work to support mine went unnoticed.

She was the one who read my early drafts and gave me notes on how to soften my pretensions. She was affiliated with me, which was its own gift. And her sense of artistic urgency centered on her teaching. The creative act of inspiring others to create, is how she put it. She taught about openness.

To live in joy, to live in the light.

To see the light even in the dark shadows.

To live a life without shadows was an errand of fools.

And yet, who could not look upon fools and envy them their frivolity?

Helen interrupted my reverie. It was she who spoke now, with more urgency. Yes, they were her words, not mine, although I felt them in my body.

Calling forth a car on the road. It's approaching the bus.

The woman's hand is outside the bus window, waving goodbye.

There are all the women's hands, waving from the bus, as they leave, as they go away forever.

Calling forth the bus driver, who sees the incoming car approaching the bus.

Calling forth the energy between them. The women's hands. The car approaching.

Calling forth the moment when the car hits the bus head-on.

The car hits the bus, with the women in it.

The women who ruined your life are in there. They're all in the bus. And it's on fire.

Breathe deep, into your body.

Calling forth fire.

Calling forth the fire, which consumes them all.

Calling forth the fire, which burns away the things we must reject. It burns and it cleanses, at the same time. This fire is beautiful. And it consumes you.

I opened my eyes. It had become too hot.

Feel the fire. Isn't it beautiful, baby?

And yet the heat was real, it was closing in on my body. I opened my eyes.

Helen was holding the fire in her hands. A bowl of fire, over me.

You made this! You made this fire with the heat of your body!

All of this was inside you, and look, now it's outside of you!

I saw my wife's face. Her hair was long, like in the beginning. She was asking me something, pleading. I could feel her hair, I was able to touch her. I recognized the softness, the feeling of feathers. Her face was framed, then it became further and further away. She was departing. She was on a train, looking at me from the window.

Water, I needed water.

The fire would consume her, it would lick her up and down like a demon.

But I broke free. I felt the dog at my feet, and then I was up, lunging for the window. I was breaking the window with a piece of metal.

I was breaking the glass.

To save her.

ACT 5

WIFE

Say you were a woman who married a man who was once your mentor. Say he was inspiring at first, but ultimately a disappointment. Say he had ideas that ran counter to your ideas. Say you had given up a lot in service to these ideas.

No.

Start over.

Say you were a man.

Right, that's much better. Say you were a man.

Say you were a man who wrote about a woman in search of meaning.

Imagine that you wrote a book that had been widely praised because it was so relatable and yet touched a nerve that was rarely reachable. Then imagine another writer wrote a book with a similar idea and it eclipsed your book, only it was a more violent version of a person's search for truth. The media couldn't stop comparing the two of you, and suddenly, you who had been this visionary were now seen as a hack, because you had been writing *about* women, but the other writer *was* a woman.

But how unfair to be judged only because of this juxtaposition to another writer. And say your books had nothing in common, really, save for their ambition to say some useful things about life. Say yours was a third-person narrative about a woman coming to terms with the horrors of the world, and the other writer's was in first person about a woman who hated other women as well as herself. In her story, say men were vulgar and society in general was to be mistrusted. No narrator, no character, was reliable, a trick the writer played on the reader, with whom she wasn't in solidarity. Reading her work was like encountering a jack in the box that popped out at the end of the final chapter, punched you in the nose, and cried: Joke's on you! Whereas yours was like a gentle reminder, the lapping of waves...

Say you read every review of this writer's book over and again and each time were filled with an annoyance bordering on rage. But not everything was about comparison and jealousy—say you told this to yourself. Say you were bothered by the idea that this writer, who you—as a man who loved women—felt was actually dangerous to women, that she was usurping the language of women, of their struggles, using it to stoke up more struggle, and say you were enraged that she was considered some sort of creative sage who had managed to tap into a secret of all humanity that, so far, had remained elusive. And while on a sentence level you could agree the woman had style and was willing to take risks, imagine you felt there to be a level of acceptance and celebration around her ideas that irked you by its very consistency, as if there were an unspoken agreement among reviewers that this woman was off limits to critique.

Maybe you even came up with a theory as to why. First, say you thought it was the writer's approach to her craft. Each of her books (pretend there were more than just the one) seemed to be predicated on some dare she had given herself, a challenge that seemed less about a magical current coursing through her than a careerist attempting to achieve prolificity. Say each of the writer's anecdotes around her process succeeded in raising her further atop her pedestal of ingenuity, as if her genius could never be replicable. But few people, if any, seemed to inquire if these structural challenges served as a shield against future failure. Say your theory was that she would debase her own process right up front so others couldn't devalue it first. That she only wanted to *appear* oppressed, to use the terms favored by those inclined to proclamations about the so-called struggle of being a woman, to be both the backbone of the broken back and the metal bar giving the beating.

Say you were a nice man who cared about people. Say you had a wife, who was also a writer, and when you thought about it, when people would ask your wife about herself, she would make a self-deprecating remark, so if she failed to impress, she would have already proven her unworthiness to herself. Pretend you saw her do this, and even though it saddened you, it was clearly a way she felt she could retain a modicum of power. And, say you considered it more generously since women had been judged harshly throughout history and had learned to judge themselves harshly, say you thought it would make sense for a woman like this writer—a woman not that different from your wife—to approach her own success with a similar distrust. Say you thought she was vulnerable, that you saw her as weak, and that this weakness endeared her to you.

But even still. Say while you were generous with your support for other writers (so generous that you felt you spent too much time helping them and didn't keep enough for yourself), say the woman writer you were always compared to seemed not to read anyone at all, actually, as if she were a blank slate, singular and pure. And that she criticized you. Say she had no circle of artists with whom she shared her work, say she refused to endorse other people's books, say she refused to ally herself with anyone at all. As if she were her own island, which would have made *you* lonely, but which only seemed to elevate her cachet.

Say this woman had been given the status of a thought leader, unable to be sullied by old ideas, who explored the darker parts of the human psyche in only "new" ways, but say you knew she was not, in fact, subversive, that there had been other women writers who called attention in more heartfelt ways to the human condition and the systems of power that sought to dominate the weak in service of the powerful. Say you wanted the media to shed a little of that light on them, too, to show that this writer being a woman with guts wasn't, in fact, such a transgressive act, and that other women had been brilliant and obscene for decades! But say you couldn't come up with many examples.

Say you said all this, published essays about it, and say you were punished for it, even though, in many ways, you were right. Because, after all, you're a man, and say—this is hypothetical—say you were reacting in part out of spite, out of envy for her success. One day, pretend you realized that your anger was likely a misplacement of your dissatisfaction with your own life, a projection of your own disquiet, your own lack of success, your discomfort with the changing implications of your own career.

And yet, as true as this might have felt, say you were still convinced that it was also possible that the woman writer was a red herring created by the male-driven collective unconscious (of which you were a part, but a less toxic part) to throw society off the scent of entrenched systems that were useful to those in power, writers like you (but not you!).

Say you wrote an essay about how this writer was a safe outlaw, and that getting behind her wasn't to join a revolution but to keep any real revolution from beginning. Say you wrote about how this writer's characters were misanthropic, how her narratives sought to destroy the people they saw as weak, that the reader was never invited to identify with her characters to better give them the illusion of a liberation from their own worst impulses. Her readers were not challenged, because the writer never challenged herself, not really, not on a human level, not on the level of *her* true nature, reserving her challenges for the laboratory of her craft. And that this was a tool to keep readers from truth.

Say her readers were therefore encouraged to have contempt for her characters, and therefore humanity in all its imperfection, to spit upon all such figures who might cross their path, flipping through her pages with great enthusiasm but little purpose. And because this woman writer had been celebrated by the literary establishment, say you wrote in this hypothetical piece of yours that the reader of her work might well come to think, "I can enjoy this violence. I can be violent too." Say you wrote that the reader was offered a stage for the performance of their desire to continue hating women and for women to continue hating themselves, which only gave the men in power and the women who serve as their handmaidens another useful tool to continue their monopoly of ideas. This woman writer, you might say, asked us to put readers seeking truth in the same category as readers who found pleasure in picking their scabs, as if bringing oneself to orgasm was the same as cutting oneself. Say you wrote that in an essay, that you titled it something witty, ironic even, but no one thought it was funny at all. Say they didn't understand your point.

Say you said this writer did not position herself as one of the people, that she was a fraud. And then you spent years consumed with anger about her. But then, even though you knew you were right, say you became tired of being so angry. Say you began to wonder what bone you had to pick with this resistance, anyway, what was it to you, what did you want? To become immortalized? To escape the disdain of the public? To make lots of money, to buy sports cars so as to drape over them in photographs and discuss ideas about the world? Say you asked yourself these questions in the shower, in the bath, on your walk to work, on your walk back home.

There is much to be said about a society that places value on a writer like this woman as someone representing progress. If anything, you would think she offered society the space to question its own attachment to genius as a commodity that could be controlled by the media in order to sell the newest version of empire. If all this woman writer was really doing was playing a game with society, asking us to idolize her while enjoying how stupid she made us look, then in hindsight you might say she did a wonderful job. Say you wondered if her career had been a performance all along, and not the one you thought it had been. Maybe her purpose was not to write great books with many universes inside them but books that exposed the universes outside of them, books that exposed us by forcing *us* to identify with something horrible that she had created, that was meant as a mirror for us. And that you had played into it and exposed your own ambition, your own desire, in all its qualifications, and that she had wanted you to.

Say you found you had no more use for these kinds of systems or even for the conversations about breaking them down. Say you wanted to read and write books about lichen, instead. Say you asked yourself, what if I moved away from critique and instead realized that this writer *was* a genius, and that a country needed geniuses for nation building? And that most geniuses are manufactured, and true geniuses are often misinterpreted, if they exist at all?

Say you died in the middle of all this hypothetical thinking. Say you died and you were living and dying at a time when no one could attend funerals. Say your obituary talked mostly of the fact that you used to take long walks with your many small dogs, and that you had inspired the world's children to become better. Say if you had rated your life based on inner harmony and affection, you would have gotten a ten, but if you had rated it based on authority and creative power, you would have gotten a five. Would this have been enough, a ten and a five?

Say you never knew because you died without knowing you were going to die. But what if you had tried to consider these concepts in the way you had always considered the role of genius in cultural transformation, if you had considered it before you died, spent time dissecting it, laying all the pieces out on the table, picking them up one by one, looking at them closely, then rearranging them. What if you had said, my small dogs and I will go down a new path today, one that is harder to find, harder to follow, steeper and covered with slippery leaves. Say before you died you had gone down that path with your small dogs and you had discovered a cave, and in that cave was a woman who could reveal the meaning of life.

Say you spent time in the cave with the woman and she had given you a prediction, that your life would end, that no one would be able to attend your funeral, that there would be no oration or reflection on your life and spirit, that for witnesses you would only have flowers, and that you would have an obituary that referred more to your many small dogs than to your genius.

Would it have been better to not have reached the cave, to not have known how it would have ended for you? Or would you have rather died having found the cave, died knowing that you would die a ten and a five, but that the ten was the more important number? Or would you have longed to make the five into a ten, too, so you could die a ten and a ten? Or would you have made your five a ten and your ten a five, if you could have, reversing them? Would you have traded your many small dogs in order that the five become a ten? Would you have consulted the flowers? Hypothetically.

ACT 6

MAN AND WIFE

I was back home. I was back in the city. Back in my apartment. It was morning. I searched around in the covers for her body.

I kissed her awake.

I was so happy to see her, as if I hadn't seen her in a lifetime. Time had passed, but how much time? I did not understand time as linear. It was possible I had gone backward, or perhaps forward, only to arch back—not at the beginning point, but just in front of it. The same latitude, but a longitude off by degrees.

It was our bed, the bed we shared, the bed in the city. It was the same mattress we had bought together on a Sunday, the floor model. The window was the same, as was the light that shone in, on my face, in the morning, that morning—the same morning but a different one.

What had changed—for something had. But time had moved so unpredictably, so that I was unable to pick out a pattern. The lamp—the same. A white ceramic base, in the shape of an amphora. The pull cord, small metal balls suspended on a line. My books were there, stacked in order of when they were to be read. The porcelain tumbler containing one pen, two mechanical pencils, and a highlighter. My headlamp, in the same position as when I had left, the strap hanging partly off the edge of the night table. She hated when I read too late, and often complained that I had become a night owl.

But these thoughts, the accounts of my life as I lived it, were from the now of *before*. The memory of that time, in a way, that I had somehow circled back to, on the same latitude but a longitude off by degrees. It wasn't that I was looking back, but rather that I was looking inward, and the memory of the behind was, in fact, within. Time didn't pass, I realized. It burrowed. And my life had not been moving in a line, but as a dark, coiled shell, encircling itself and tightening with time. It was this dark shell I was in, but I knew it only as morning, as the time of awakening.

And so, because it was all I knew, I entered it gladly, as anyone would, with the light of day on their face and the feeling of a warm limb adjacent, under a mound of covers. If only I could get to her...

Led by her scent, I found the arc of her thigh and I followed it up to her stomach and chest, then her neck, and I popped my head out of the covers and licked her face. It was a new kind of ritual, a joyful intimacy. I had seen myself do it before but had never *experienced* it. In the space of now, that was on a longitude with then, but whose latitude was off by degrees, I had seen myself embark on the same quest to find her breath and breathe it, too, to kiss her when her guard was down, to remind her of my presence through an ebullience that endeared her to me, without fail, every time, despite the judgments I could see being made that my love was too abrupt, that it was all about me, that I was awake, whereas she had to be roused by me from her docile state.

Nevertheless, seeing my own enthusiasm in this way was surprising, despite the feeling that I had seen it before, many times. Because I had seen it before, but I had never *felt* it. I had seen myself hurl myself on top of her body, lick her face. I had seen myself wriggle with pleasure.

She turned her head away.

I had seen that, too. I had seen it for too long—this flinching at my touch, as if it were a reminder of her own body, which she had been trying to forget. And yet this time, she turned her head back. She held my face in her two hands and tugged on my ears lovingly.

I was excited. She touched me. I was back—back in my bed, in the city, in the apartment we shared. She was awake, too. She tenderly rubbed my ear. I couldn't wait. I threw myself over her, draping on her heavily, like a damp towel being tossed over the back of a chair.

Oh no you don't.

She pushed me aside.

But this was home to me. I had seen it, and I was back. Something had changed, but the light had remained. Maybe this was why I stayed up late, to enter into the world of mystery that sleep protected us from so well—the despairing, endless hours between late and dawn—bending the laws of physics. Always, though, after staying up, I would fall asleep eventually, and I would awaken convinced I had only slept for an hour, but there was a chance it had been five.

She got out of bed, put on her robe and went to the kitchen. This, too, I had become familiar with, this daily act of rejecting me. I had felt it for years. Her getting up early to make the coffee, then do her exercises. She was a morning person, which was one of the tallied incompatibilities which made up part of her case against marriage. I would lay in half sleep, knowing I should follow her, but fearing the transition between dawn and day.

After first hesitating, like every morning, I followed her. Almost jauntily, even through the fog of getting up after not enough sleep, feeling embarrassed for wanting to waste time in bed, and yet with purpose, a kind of presence. That day I was refreshed. It was different, as if I had slept for days. I was fully expectant and enlivened. I was brand new. I shook myself and I heard the sound.

Perhaps it was the feeling of one more chance. The world giving me a choice to love. It had been love I was looking for, the only real thing. The thing I had been searching for was, in fact, just within reach, and had been there all along. It was just that I had to move through time in a different way to return to it.

I entered the kitchen.

The smell was so familiar, the odor of brewing coffee, that metallic, hollow crrrrrrr as the liquid in the moka pot sprayed from the steamer rod. She removed the coffee from the burner. I sat on the couch and settled into the cushion, curled up, to wait.

She brought her cup over. She sat with me in the chair. These were such beautiful moments where speech was not needed; we were only bodies, caring for one another. She put her arm around me and stroked my head.

Baby.

She pulled on my ear again, and she moved the coffee to her mouth.

So soft.

I put my head into her neck. She smelled like the sea, like running in circles, like collapsing as the water flattens on the sand. I couldn't resist her skin, as if I had never been so close to her. Love, it was what I was after! To awaken with the woman who had been there the whole time, but whose love I had to spiral and tighten to get to. I had to fossilize to an extent before I could see her. I had to become something else entirely, so that I could appreciate her. So that she could appreciate me! And so that I could taste her!

Oh my god, her skin was salty and sweet, it was musky and clean, it had the taste of warmth and roundness. It was so delicious. I gave it a small bite. I bit her on her lips, as if eating her. A small bite, as I wanted, in that moment, to consume her.

Forget about love. I wanted to enter her completely, through my body, on top of her body, membrane to membrane.

Bad baby.

No bite.

I knew then to stop.

I sat back in the chair, and she drank her coffee and stared at her phone. What was in there, I wondered. What sick thrills could captivate such a smell as hers, so that she doubled over, her shoulders hunched, oblivious to the light coming in from the window. That warm, rectangular pocket of light as it hit the floor. A white shadow of pure light.

She asked if I wanted breakfast.

I wanted so badly to be taken care of. I was a child, a baby. I had that baby inside me still. I had been burrowing and burrowing into myself, and here I was, a baby. I had been going further and further inward in time, and now I was older, but it was the same container. Just coiled around and around itself, ossified, but still gooey at the center, the springy scum of muscle and cells, attainable but contained by shell, and I was surrounding it again and again, meeting back at the same point but spreading in incremental reverberations...

And I was hungry! Desperate to eat!

How long since she had given me the gift of a meal in the morning? To eat, next to such pockets of light, the way it warmed through the window. Her smell. The light. The lingering taste of her mouth. The feeling of it in my teeth, the way her lip felt when I lowered my quivering jaw and the smell of the sheets after she left them, the duvet with her scent, the window and the wall just completely bathed in light, the window open just enough to hear the chorus of birds already communicating. And the food, she put it on my dish and I heard it, and it thrilled me, to see this woman move around the kitchen in such grace, bathed by that late season light, by those shadows.

Sit.

I did what she said, and I knew it would make her happy.

Good baby.

It was the way she said it, it felt so familiar. I knew that this moment, the moment of morning, of light, of her neck, of her lips and the buoyancy with which I bit them, the smell of coffee and breakfast, the smell of saltwater, of sand, her eyes, her hands—all this was infinite. And yet, it was fleeting. I had to embrace its infiniteness just as I was seeing it to completion.

The hours passed. She sat at a table, using pen and paper. She spoke to herself every so often.

Start over.

Say you were a woman.

No, say you were a man.

Say you started over.

I saw her get up, make tea.

She prepared a light snack of cheese, olives, and popcorn. My treasure. She offered me kernel after kernel, placing each on my tongue.

Then, the clattering of spoon in sink, followed by more sitting, more stretching, and writing.

I fell asleep to the sound of her working. She was scratching at the paper for hours, for so many stretches of light, and the light moved around, from her table to her shoulders, then onto me. And I bathed in it, soaked in sunlight, yellowing on my cheek. I had never been so drunk on light, so lazy.

We took a walk together, outside, in the sun. She talked to me. She remarked on my body, how special I was, how naughty. She told me I was sweet, and that I was just a bit naughty. She told me I could stop and smell whatever I wanted. That it was okay for me to be there, to wade in the water, to feel it on my feet.

We went back up to the apartment. The light was fading. It had thinned and lost the yellow. She gave me dinner. She rubbed my ears for a while, on the couch.

So cute. My baby.

I rescued you. And now you're mine.

I let her say it. I was tiny, and she could say it.

I put my face down, on her leg.

This book is printed with plant-based inks on materials certified by the Forest Stewardship Council®. The FSC® promotes an ecologically, socially and economically responsible management of the world's forests.
This book has been printed without the use of plastic-based coatings.

The authorized representative in the EEA is eucomply OÜ, Pärnu mnt 139b-14, 11317 Tallinn, Estonia.
hello@eucompliancepartner.com
+337 576 90241

Fitzcarraldo Editions
133 Rye Lane
London, SE15 4ST
United Kingdom

Copyright © Makenna Goodman, 2026
Originally published in the United Kingdom
by Fitzcarraldo Editions in 2026

The right of Makenna Goodman to be identified as the
author of this work has been asserted in accordance with
Section 77 of the Copyright, Designs and Patents Act 1988.

ISBN 978-1-80427-220-6

Design by Ray O'Meara
Typeset in Fitzcarraldo
Printed and bound by Pureprint

All rights reserved. No part of this publication may be reproduced,
stored in a retrieval system or transmitted in any form or
by any means, electronic, mechanical, photocopying,
recording or otherwise, without prior permission
in writing from Fitzcarraldo Editions.

Without in any way limiting the author's exclusive rights
under copyright, any use of this publication to 'train'
generative artificial intelligence (AI) technologies to
generate text is expressly prohibited. The author
reserves all rights to license uses of this work
for generative AI training and development
of machine learning language models.

fitzcarraldoeditions.com

Fitzcarraldo Editions